THE U[illegible] OF

FLORA COTTON

TRACEE FINDLATER

LYRIA BOOKS

First published in Great Britain in 2025
Lyria Books

A CIP Catalogue of this book is available from the British Library

ISBN 978-0-9932463-2-6 (Paperback)

Cover and typesetting by
www.chandlerbookdesign.com

Printed in Great Britain by
TJ Books, Padstow, Cornwall

'The feelings that hurt most, the emotions that sting most, are those that are absurd – the longing for impossible things, precisely because they are impossible; nostalgia for what never was.'

Fernando Pessoa

CONTENTS

PART ONE

GHOSTS IN THE LIBRARY

1

There's a café across the road from the library where I sit before work, lingering over a cup of coffee. I've done this every day since it happened. I like the idea that the staff know my name and my order. They greet me as I arrive, shaking the rain from my hair or grumbling about whatever delayed me. The mood is always warm and welcoming, the kind of place where someone might compliment me on my new coat. I'll shrug it off with a smile and say, 'This old thing? I've had it for years!' And we'll laugh, because isn't life just hilarious?

To be honest, this never happens. Both my drink and I are instantly forgettable. The most I manage by way of interaction is to rush out my order before scuttling for the window seat – the spear carrier who got one line in the play only to fluff it. I sit alone, looking out at the sandstone library, misplaced among its brick and concrete neighbours, and wonder what I might have said if small talk didn't feel like such an effort.

Perhaps tomorrow, when the cheerful woman with the colourful headscarf is taking orders, I'll try again. Of course, that version of tomorrow will never arrive. It is always today.

It's been three weeks since The Black Eyed Boy left me, which means three long weeks of trying not to think about his distant eyes and crooked smile. I haven't had much success. For instance, when I'm at work, I'll be shelving a book or switching off a computer and realise I've been on autopilot, lost in thoughts of him – what he's doing, if he's thinking about me at the same moment I'm thinking about him. It's ridiculous, really. I'm sure I'm the last thing on his mind.

That's what I'm doing now, forcing him out of my head to focus on the task at hand as I push the book trolley out of the lift onto the basement floor (Science and Technology). The trolley has a wonky wheel and veers left if I don't pay attention. Since my thoughts tend to wander, I have to make an effort.

The basement is the least interesting of the three floors in the library, a windowless rectangle with the lift at one end and stairs at the other, neat metal rows thrown into cold indifference by flickering strip lights. It's not exactly eerie, but there's an emptiness that seeps into you, especially when it's quiet.

Two years ago, when I started working at the library, it was busier. There used to be enough people around to keep my afternoon shifts ticking along. Now, time seems stretched. Fewer readers come and go, more desk-squatters plug in to watch TV shows on the public computers. It's still a nice place to work, a gothic-style building with a leaky roof and a layout that only makes sense when you choose to love its quirks. There's talk about moving to a converted car park in town, making it some sort of information centre with an atrium and a Costa. I'd rather that didn't happen. I'm used to it, so there's no need for change.

Today there's an additional weight in the air that makes me pause. I hear the lift doors slide back, then nothing, as if all sound is about to disappear from the world. Unless I'm overthinking.

I consider saying something out loud, just to be sure, when the wayward trolley catches on the edge of a carpet tile, dislodging two oversized cookbooks. I lean in to catch them, but end up turning them awkwardly as they slide through my fingertips. Sound is restored with a muffled *thud-um* as the books land askew on the floor. Everything else catches up then, the world resuming its usual hum, and I hear the old-style wall clock making its furious tick, so disgusted by time that it spits it out bitterly.

I tidy as I do my last restock of the afternoon, picking up crisp wrappers and discarded half pencils. I once found a used syringe – something that had been mentioned in the induction training, improbable as it sounds, so that was exciting. I had to cordon off the area until someone from the council came to deal with it, and spent the whole waiting hour wondering who would turn up. Would there be hazmat suits? Perhaps someone from the local paper tagging along? It turned out to be the cranky guy from Estates, who picked up the syringe in some toilet roll and threw it in the wheelie bin out back. A bit of a letdown. I could have done that. It was clear he thought the same.

Before this, I had a factory job for a few months, straight out of school. It was a bit monotonous, moving cans of beans and macerated fruits around, although I didn't mind as I met The Black Eyed Boy there. He worked in the kitchens, and I loved it when he would come home in a haze of chilli and smoked paprika.

'You'll turn orange!' he'd say with playful resistance when I put my arms around him to take in his fiery warmth.

For a moment, I feel that glow lingering in the air, catch the shape of him clearly in my mind: the tilt of his head, the brush of his hair, the soft weight of his hands. It shifts out of reach quickly, fading into the memory of him dragging his duffle bag through the hallway, leaving behind an apology that barely disturbed the silence around it.

I find yet another abandoned pencil in one of the rows of science books. It's only when I bend to pick it up that I notice something else below the bottom shelf, maybe a coin glinting in the fluorescent shimmer. I kneel and use the pencil to flick it out. It's not a coin but an origami star made from a silver sweet wrapper, its edges neatly folded.

I hold the star in the palm of my hand, and it fits perfectly in the indent. The light catching in the folds isn't the fake light of a fluorescent tube, but distant, brilliant starlight. The strange light imprints itself on my eyes, and I see out beyond to that very system: the civilisations that are built there, vast technological super-structures sitting alongside ancient megaliths, intricate airborne machines flitting like fireflies in an indigo –

'Flora?'

I blink away the daydream and step out into the aisle, pushing the star into the pocket of my oversized cardigan. Lilly is waiting on the stairs, her eyes impatient beneath the thick cat flick of her eyeliner as she adjusts a strand of hair trying to escape from a high victory roll. Lilly is the librarian, my boss, and she never stays late.

'It's five to six and the last one's out. I'm going to lock up.'

I look at my trolley and reckon I have about fifteen minutes of shelving left to do.

'I'll be a few minutes.'

'Are you okay to let yourself out? I need to get away.'

'No problem. See you tomorrow.'

It's the usual exchange. Lilly knows I'll be here for a while yet and I know that she's pushing her luck by leaving early. It's never commented on, that would break our quiet complicity.

I'm happy to be in the library by myself, although there are certain things I don't do. First, I prefer not to be in the basement and get upstairs as soon as I can. Second, I never get in the lift when I'm alone. That's just practicality. I can't imagine the cranky guy from Estates being thrilled to come in out of hours to help some poor sod who got stuck in the lift. That's if I'd even been able to alert anyone – it's such a shonky old thing, I doubt the alarm even works.

Every evening, I put the empty trolley in the lift and take the stairs to meet it. The ground floor is the heart of the building. There's fiction behind the service desk (mostly crime and historical romance: we have an ageing population), along with reference materials and a small audio section. It's nicer than the basement, with a mezzanine first floor that circles all the way around, so the ceiling is way up high.

As I reach the top of the stairs, I notice that Lilly has left the main light on for me. It illuminates only the centre of this floor, leaving the shelves beyond shrouded in darkness. I suppose it might seem pretty spooky, a public building with no one else around, but I like it. There are evenings when I'll spend hours on the top floor alone, reading my book or browsing the travel section, dreaming about all the places that I'll never get to. I might even bring in a Pot Noodle, make a night of it. It's not as if I've got anything to get home to these days.

I flick off the basement light switch and head towards the lift. The way the central light favours the area around the service desk means the path I follow falls between light and darkness; there's a definite edge to the luminescence, like a spotlight on a stage.

Perhaps it's this sense of theatre that makes me feel uneasy all of a sudden. Not as if I'm being watched exactly, but not *not* that either. It's one of those old feelings, moving leaves suggesting a tiger in the bushes. Or is it the wind and I'm imagining the tiger?

'Hello?'

The darkness consumes my call, making my voice sound unfamiliar. I feel a little silly, unnerved. What is it? I've wandered to the lift a hundred times along this border of darkness, pulled out the trolley and stored it by the desk ready for tomorrow. Why is today different?

'Lilly, are you here?'

My voice doesn't crackle with fear, only a slight tremble. If anything, I sound cross, like I won't be happy to end up the butt of some childish joke.

It's not until I'm nearly at the lift that I realise what's out of place. Someone has already removed the trolley. It waits, innocuous yet uncanny, outside the lift door.

I hate it in horror films when a lone would-be victim spends too long gazing in astonishment at something amiss, leaving time for someone to creep up behind them, appear in front and terrorise them, or otherwise make escape impossible. Even though nothing like this has ever happened to me before, I react quickly – and not like a horror heroine. In fact, the experience splits me in two: the rational part of my brain is saying, *okay, Flora, this is a bit weird, but we can just leave calmly*, while the emotional side is screaming, *ohmygodgetoutgetoutgetout*!

Strangely, the rational side takes over, forcing me to focus on the light of here and now and not what might be lurking in the shadows. Yes, my heartbeat pulses to my head as I grab my coat from the staff room. Yes, the key shakes in my hand as I lock the door behind me and descend the steps at a brisk pace. I'm also holding my breath, not that I notice until I reach the bottom and have to exhale hard. Considering the trolley appeared to have moved out of the lift *by itself*, I've done pretty well.

I decide to take the long route home. I normally walk through the park, as it's right across the road from the library and not much further to my house on the other side. The alternative takes twice as long, winding past a parade of shops and bars, then across a couple of busy roads.

With the sensation of blood pumping, I need a longer walk, to be safe under the streetlights and cocooned by the traffic noise. I try not to rush, smoothing my hair as I catch my reflection in the dark window of a passing bus, convincing myself I look composed.

My breath is almost back to normal as I turn onto the parade. Most of the shops are closed now, but the convenience store is still open, as well as the Indian restaurant and the burger bar. With a few other people milling around, I could believe I was overreacting about the trolley. There will be a logical explanation; there has to be.

I'm on the verge of accepting this, and even consider a takeaway for dinner, when a familiar silhouette ahead catches my eye: the way he moves towards me, that languid gait beneath the streetlights, skinny legs planted in oversized boots scuffing along the pavement.

The Black Eyed Boy.

I call him that because my mum used to call him The Blue Eyed Boy in a semi-ironic way, as I appeared incapable of finding any fault with him. It's a fitting modification now because, when I think of him, I picture a shark. Those night-dark eyes don't scheme or hate, they just don't care.

My breath hitches. The rational part of my brain makes another attempt to step in, but it goes something like, *okay, Flora, you're much better than –*

I miss the end of that thought because I've ducked, or more accurately dived, into the narrow alley at the side of the electrical shop, just in time for my ex-boyfriend to pass. He is striding along, carefree and oblivious as ever, headphones on, and I'm crouching among a pile of bin bags spilling out a week's worth of rubbish and their assorted aromas.

Brilliant!

If I was ever unsure which was scarier – ghosts in the library or running into my ex – I've got my answer now.

2

Thursday morning. I'm painting the hallway of my house a greyish shade of pink. It complements the deep rose I chose for the woodwork when I decided that, if I'm going to be stuck here alone, it might as well be pretty.

As I paint, I daydream that The Black Eyed Boy wishes he'd never left and begs to come back. We've agreed on a time for him to move his stuff back in, but when the time comes, I don't open the door when he knocks. The knocking turns to desperate banging, like he's being pursued, and I roll emulsion up and down the wall, feeling my work intensify with the rising weight of his despair.

When I was about eight, I watched *The Heiress* with my Aunt Bette, which must have influenced this particular moment, since I caught the end of it on TV last night. In my mind, that is exactly what is happening now: the creation of pretty pink walls, colours he would surely despise, my way of blowing out the candles and leaving him out in the rain.

When he left, I found out that he'd been seeing a girl from work behind my back for almost a year. I call her 21 and Blonde because her real name would put me off being civil to anyone with the same name. I've been in turn annoyed with him for his deceit, annoyed with myself for my weakness, annoyed with her for her appeal and then round again in a series of nauseating circles.

Sometimes I sit in a bar drinking rosé with my best friend as we plot a delicious revenge involving spiked cocktails and a crypto scam. Only I don't have a best friend, I can't stand rosé, and I wouldn't know how to plot revenge if my life depended on it. Just another daydream.

The memory of seeing him last night adds vigour to my work. It's not that I'd lost the sense of his presence, but I was getting used to there being a gap instead of an actual person. To be reminded of him so plainly didn't feel good. To be reminded of all the hopes that vanished when he did – the sense of having someone to get through life's tasks with, a companion for the small adventures that would sustain us – was even worse. I never thought someone so content in front of the TV would end up finding it all so tedious.

I hate the way he continues to wander around in my head, even as I try to paint him out.

I make a mess of resting the roller on the tray because the letterbox rattles, and I jump as the latest postcard from my mum drops onto the mat. It's a picture of Edinburgh riverside at night, gabled buildings lit by a chain of golden lights, all reflecting themselves in the motionless water. It's reminiscent of a town from one of the stories she used to tell me when I was little.

I miss her voice and think fleetingly about calling her. It's been so long since we talked that I haven't even told her about the breakup. I can't bear the thought of how pleased she'll be, and the lengths she'll go to disguise it – all those drawn-out notes of concern while secretly glad that it's over.

'If things don't work out, you know where to find me.'

The memory of her saying this is vivid. Another of her gift-wrapped hand grenades.

Still, I fiddle with my phone for a while, hovering over the call button. She's probably annoyed that I haven't returned her calls, and will do that thing she does with silence, waiting for me to do all the talking.

It's been six months since she left, but I had my Black Eyed Boy, told her I was happy. Then he left too.

I eat granola for lunch, at the counter in my narrow kitchen, a galley that leads out to an even narrower backyard. Now that the hallway looks nice, I'm aware of how grim the yellowed paint is in here, how dusty the corners are once you get your eye in, and how that grey patch beside the sink is much worse than I thought.

I distract myself with the origami star I found in the basement yesterday. It's bent out of shape, having spent the night in my pocket. I lay it on the counter and smooth out the creases. It's a sweet thing, and I'm caught briefly in its radiant shimmer before remembering what happened last night.

In the light of day, the moving trolley seems pretty fanciful, even by my standards. I must have dawdled coming up the stairs, which coincided with Lilly getting distracted. Maybe a phone call – that would be it. Taking the trolley out of the lift must have been Lilly's last, exasperated task before she too hurried out into the night.

Thursday is the busiest day as it's when the mobile library is loaded and unloaded. The loading happens in the morning, when I'm not here, but it usually comes back around three o'clock. Whoever is on the floor – usually me – has to drop everything to unload the books so the van can move on. It's early today, and I'm lugging piles of books from the van before I've even taken my coat off.

The trolley sits in its usual spot beside the service desk. I can't help giving it a sideways look before I start organising the books onto it. There's no sign that anything untoward has happened. I don't get the sense it's become a "cursed" trolley, and I don't feel that gnawing dread you get from a horror film. I'm happy to stick with my conclusion that Lilly was here late. That's all there is to it. It's a sunny day, with dust motes dancing in the sunbeams and an array of hardbacks and large-print romances waiting to be put away.

Today I'm working with Cal, who sits at the service desk while I do the shelving. He's a nice guy with the look of an old-school science teacher, all elbow patches and corduroy flares, messy salt-and-pepper hair. As far as possible, he likes to confine himself to the audio section. He's really into vinyl and will somehow bring it into almost any conversation.

I begin in the fiction section, a maze that reels out behind the service desk, dotted with barrel chairs and the odd study table. I enjoy it on a day like today because there's a big stained glass window at the back of the building that shines in strips of red and yellow, making you feel as though you're finding your way through some medieval quest. I don't love it as much as my favourite floor, which is upstairs, but on a sunny day, the warmth and colour are uplifting.

'Excuse me.'

Mrs Barker, a library regular, stops me. She's a brisk sort of person, earnest about what she wants in a way that can often seem amusing. She once told me she was looking for *The Solar System*. I was going to tell her it was all around her, but you have to pick your battles.

'I'm looking for *The Right Man*,' she says.

'A novel?' I ask, twisting my lips to halt a rising smirk, resisting the obvious.

'It's a biography of Isaac Newton.'

'It'll be in the basement. Do you want me to go and fetch it for you?'

'Would you mind? With your young legs, you'll be much quicker than me.'

My "young legs" are a standing joke around here. The lift doesn't go to the first floor, so my being a good deal younger than most of the other staff means they tend to leave piles of books for me and my "young legs" to lug up the stairs.

The basement is cold as usual and almost deserted, a single person in one of the rows. Typically, they're in the Science section, where I need to be.

'I'm sorry –' I begin to say as I approach the row, assuming I'm about to get in someone's way. As it turns out, the moment unfolds very differently to how I expect. My apology remains unfinished.

It will become difficult to remember how it went – how it really went. The gist is this: someone was standing there, then they were not. They were holding a book, a hardback physics textbook. I know this because, as soon as I step into the row, the book drops. Five feet. Straight to the floor.

At first, I do nothing. My rational self, backed by my sense of responsibility to a customer, slowly takes control, despite the glaring lack of explanation. I force a hard inhale, ignoring the chill blooming beneath my ribs as I pick up the textbook and shelve it in its proper place. Then I scan the shelves for *The Right Man*, relieved that the spine's text is bold and stands out. Taking it in the crook of my arm, I turn coolly, if somewhat mechanically, out into the aisle and make my way upstairs. By the time I hand the book to Mrs Barker, you'd never know anything strange had just happened. My hands are shaking a bit, but that could be from exertion.

A few weeks ago, I would have texted The Black Eyed Boy to tell him about it. He would have sent back a shocked face emoji. I'd have been excited at the prospect of elaborating over dinner, buzzing with potential theories, only to be disappointed by another text a few minutes later telling me he wouldn't be home for dinner.

Now I have no one to tell. I suppose I could tell Cal, but he's over in the audio section trying to get someone to put the headphones on and listen to a vinyl copy of *The Wall.*

I suddenly feel peevish and want to march over and tell him that no one cares about vinyl any more. In fact, most people only stumble into his stupid audio section by mistake. I imagine doing just that, Cal's expectant face falling.

Tears begin to bubble at the back of my eyes, and I reach for my phone. I want to call The Black Eyed Boy and find that the last few weeks never happened. I want to call my mum and find that she's waiting for me in the café across the road. Except I can't. Everyone is gone.

Is there a ghost in the library?

I circle back to the question as I sit in front of the TV, having finally stopped crying and gotten up from the spot on the hallway floor where I crumpled as soon as I got home.

I haven't cried much at all until now. Even when The Black Eyed Boy left, it wasn't sadness I felt, just a hollow sort of shock. What it said about me: how I'm not much fun to be around, not as attractive as other girls. There was no breakdown, no tearful reckoning. I went on. Alone. I'm an only child, so solitude isn't something I mind. Today, though, I felt it – something interesting happened, and there was no one to tell.

This is the second evening in a row I've come straight home from work instead of lingering on the library's top floor. I was enjoying those evenings hidden among the books. I miss it. Now there seems to be something else there. Whether I'm imagining it or not, I don't think I can handle it.

I'm halfway through a Pot Noodle and a rerun of *Law & Order* when it hits me: something strange or supernatural could happen anywhere. Even here, at home in my terraced house, with the lights on and the heating humming, wouldn't a creaky floorboard or a flicker in the corner of my eye feel just as unnerving as it would in the library? Either way, I'm alone.

That settles it. Tomorrow I'm going to spend the evening in the library. I'll read my book and refuse to let my imagination run wild with thoughts of ghosts.

And if there is one, it'll just have to keep quiet and let me read.

3

Annoyingly, I have to spend most of Friday on the service desk because Anouska has called in sick again. Anouska has been off two weeks out of the last four, and Lilly was so frustrated by it that she said out loud that this was it for her, which she's normally too professional to do.

I never took to Anouska – she has a knack for disappearing when there's work to be done and reappearing just in time to collect the praise. I was secretly glad she got caught out, although I joined in the usual murmurs of polite regret.

The day passes without incident, and Lilly takes over the desk from five o'clock so I can finish the shelving. As I step into the lift down to the basement, my mind is mostly empty, except for the familiar thought that I have no plans for the weekend.

A fleeting, self-indulgent feeling creeps in: maybe I'm just a waste of space. No wonder The Black Eyed Boy left me. Then I imagine someone shaking him violently to discover whether any kind of emotion might present itself. It doesn't.

I normally begin with the top two floors and end in the basement. After the events of the last few days, though, I don't want today to go the same way, so I flip my route around. I have a lighter load and get through the basement by quarter past, then head to the first floor.

This is my favourite floor, a mezzanine that runs a complete circle around the main body of the library, housing all of life's beautiful things: Art, Philosophy, Literature and Travel.

At the top of the stairs, the shelves along the walls give way to a recess with a sofa, above which a round leaded window lights up the potential gloom. From outside the building, you can see that the recess is formed by a small castellated tower. Inside, it's a comfortable nook. This is where I sit when I have the place to myself, and I covet it so jealously that I physically bristle if someone else is sitting here and doesn't appear suitably reverent. When it's dark outside, the moonlight shines the window's geometric rose pattern onto the floor, and it's magical.

There's also a small hatch below the shelves to the left of the recess, which, to my knowledge, no one else has found. I don't put anything valuable in there, just a couple of books.

I've always preferred old books: they seem bigger, more to connect with. When most of my schoolmates were reading *Harry Potter,* I was racing windswept through *Wuthering Heights* or searching for *The Moonstone. I spent One Thousand and One Nights* with Scheherazade, roamed terrifying forests and dirty cobbles looking for *Dracula.* That's one of the reasons I like working here: it keeps me close to the classics.

I'm currently re-reading *The Count of Monte Cristo*, partly because it's so dense that I can lock myself away in its fortress of words, and partly because I was drawn to the idea of catching up with a character who has set out to punish wrongdoing. He's currently living in the hatch for when I stay in the library to read in the evening, which I'm planning to do once I finish my shift.

As I get about halfway around the mezzanine, I look over the balustrade to see how busy it is downstairs. There are two desk-squatters and three people at various stages of the fiction maze. In about ten minutes, Lilly will start wandering around to tell them that the library will be closing soon. Lilly can be formidable when someone threatens to keep her from leaving on time.

I sometimes wonder if Home Lilly is much different to Work Lilly, but haven't made any effort to find out. I know she lives in a village outside of town with her partner, Jen. That's about it. I don't know what their house is like. I imagine something out of a Graham Greene novel styled by Vivienne Westwood.

A ballroom. Black and white monochrome tiles over the floor with enough space to hold every sashaying skirt that sweeps its soft circles. I am one of many, whirling in synchronicity to a masquerade waltz. I don't have to think. I don't even have to feel. I just *do*. There is no sense of where the room ends, if it's a room at all because there's no ceiling, rather a midnight patchwork of sky held up by never-ending columns.

The women wear long harlequin gowns and the men embroidered waistcoats and dark tailcoats. We are all masked. My mask is plumed with a beautiful peacock feather.

I love to dance. Wherever I lived before (I can't remember where that was), I was never able to dance. Here I am pure abandon, beholden to none.

But I make one turn too many and everything spins into a blur – an unruly spinning top skidding across the table until it finally shudders and thuds to the floor. It's the thud that stirs me from my nap. Not a top, a book. My book. *The Count of Monte Cristo*, tumbling from my hand and landing askew on the floor beside the sofa.

It takes a few minutes for my sombre surroundings to resolve themselves after the dreamy colours of the ballroom. The library is in darkness except for my small lamp and the moonlit rose pattern cast upon the floor. I miss the dancing and feel its loss like a song cut off abruptly, the final note left forever unsung. I wonder if it will always be this way now, me alone in the dark, incomplete.

Somewhere inside, I can still hear the drama of the waltz playing. I stand and close my eyes, shifting to step-two-three to the left and then turning to the right-two-three. In my imagination, I can hear the music again, turning on the spot so fast that I almost lose my balance and laugh out loud.

Regaining my composure, I close my eyes once more and this time imagine another dance, something more delicate, a minuet, my right hand held out in front of me, the left over my heart. I bob with affected grace, as if greeting a gentleman, and turn my feet below an imaginary gown of pale chiffon. My hand reaches out further, a light turn of the wrist bringing up my right palm to meet another in the dark.

My eyes snap open and a man looks back at me, shimmering in the silver light from the rose window. He is tall and reaches out his left hand, pressing it against my right. I should not see him and yet he is there, as plain as the books that frame him, dressed as though part of their very fabric. His coat is that of a Victorian gentleman, dusty as an old hardback, with a necktie and collar of the same softly worn tones. His features are pale, the hollow cheeks of apparent death but with gemstone clear eyes.

'*It is but a dream, a nightmare, that has disturbed you.*'

His voice is low and resonant, carrying a bygone sincerity that modern English no longer conveys.

'The Count of Monte Cristo,' I say. I recognise the quote with certainty, though my voice comes out in a doubtful whisper. I can hear my heartbeat and feel the light hairs rising along my arms, but I remain transfixed, staring at him, too close to a dream to summon real fear.

'One of my favourite works,' he replies, motioning towards the thick paperback splayed open beside the sofa. My eyes follow his gaze and I recall waking from my dream of a masquerade, the last chapter I was reading, the Count's arrival in Rome.

'Mine too.'

Looking back, I can't stop staring at him. I don't understand his eyes, impossibly bright, but of a colour I can't attempt to catalogue: green or blue or grey or a mix of all three without being blended. How can that be, a pure colour that is nonetheless a mix of colours? Everything about him is somehow peculiar yet curiously authentic.

'I don't know who you are,' I say.

When I reflect on this later, it will seem a silly thing to have said, and I'll no doubt think of a hundred better lead-ins that would have made more sense. I'm poor at introductions and a little scared, so I went with whatever came to mind.

'No, Flora Cotton, you do not.'

A wave of confusion rolls over me, but before I can ask how he knows my name, he flashes me a collusive smile and is gone. No puff of smoke or filmic pull backwards into oblivion. He is simply no longer here.

I look over my shoulder and do a full circle in case he has moved, but I know that he is gone. I am alone again, except for the sensation of my hand being touched, living heat trying to penetrate the cold he left behind.

I'm less afraid than I know I ought to be. Surprised, obviously, but not frightened because he didn't seem all that frightening. I'm more concerned that I may have disappointed him. Maybe he saw something in me and hoped for more, as if the potential didn't quite stand up to scrutiny. Maybe I infected him with my disappointment. It would be just like me to ruin something interesting without even trying.

'I'm sorry!' I call out to no one. It's not enough, so I go down to the desk and fetch a square of memo paper to write a note. *Please come back.*

I put the note in the hidden hatch along with *The Count of Monte Cristo.* Then I take it out. This is ridiculous. I'm leaving a note for a... ghost? What kind of fool does that? What if he comes back? What if he doesn't?

After a few seconds of indecision, I put the note back in the hatch. What's the worst that can happen?

4

I would not be the right woman for a man like him. The woman for him would be as tall as he is, with an elegant fishtail skirt to her dress and a cascade of long black hair. She would carry a black parasol and make it seem perfectly acceptable to wear sunglasses indoors.

She would not spend Saturday morning lying flat on her belly, painting skirting boards in her pyjamas while old detective procedurals play on her laptop. She probably wouldn't even have a laptop. She'd have some sort of edgy phone-tablet hybrid thing that's way ahead of the curve but still classic.

I'm considering this because I fell asleep thinking about the man with the grainy voice and jewel eyes, and woke with the same thought in my head. Of course he was a dream. A figment. Let's face it, if I were to make a man out of nothing but dreams, I have no doubt he would appear much like the stranger in the library. No one quotes *The Count of Monte Cristo*. No one. I've never met anyone else who's actually read it. No one reaches out a hand to dance with a mysterious stranger without it being a fabrication.

And yet, I can still feel the sensation in my hand that he left there. So either a ghostly man is haunting the library or I'm going mad. Or a ghostly man is haunting the library *and* I'm going mad.

Something tells me this will not end well for me.

I'm drawn back to the library late on Saturday afternoon. It's growing dark outside, so it's quiet: just Cal at the service desk while a couple of desk-squatters sit transfixed by their monitors.

Cal waves when he sees me come through the door, and I mouth that I left my book upstairs, gesturing demonstratively upwards as though this might be helpful. He nods back with the same pointless vigour.

There's no one else up here, so I kneel in front of the low hatch to retrieve my paperback. I've decided to carry on reading at home because I finished the painting sooner than expected and was getting bored of watching TV – there are only so many times you can see the same formula play out without getting restless.

If I'm being honest, there's also a part of me that wants to know whether the *please come back* note is still there. Okay, it's mostly that.

I find the note *where* I left it, but not *as* I left it. It's been folded into an origami heart, resting on my paperback's cover like an insignia on the illustrated count's chest. I'm frozen in place, unable to feel my legs.

'You seem to like origami, so I made it for you.'

The stranger is standing beside me, arms folded behind his back like someone in a gallery transfixed by a painting, with that same knowing, wicked smile he left me with last night. He really is tall and reed-thin, looking at me over the curve of his aquiline nose. I shift awkwardly at the sight of him, and he holds out a hand to help me up. I just stare at it.

'Please, let me help you,' he says when it becomes clear that further instruction is required.

I hold his hand for as long as it takes to get back on my feet, then I dust myself down and reach for my book and the origami heart. I half expect him to have disappeared when I look again, but he is still there, daunting and bright-eyed as he was last night.

'Shall we sit?'

He holds his hand out to the sofa, and I sit despite myself. His height gives him elegance as he folds beside me. I feel like a squat toad by comparison – not an equal, rather some kind of familiar.

I have a barrage of questions looming. I can't think where to start, so I just sit there looking puzzled. I consider how it will look if someone comes up the stairs. Will I be talking out loud to no one?

'Anyone passing will merely see two people talking,' he says in answer to my unasked question. 'People see what they expect to see. I am as visible as I need to be.'

'Are you a mind reader?'

'I assumed you would be curious as to our circumstances.'

I nod as though I appreciate the rationality, although I'm still fighting the sensation that this is the most bizarre thing that has ever happened to me. Well, other than finding out I'd spent a year oblivious to my ex-boyfriend's affair. I certainly prefer this. As second-most-bizarre things go, this is weird but not unpleasant.

'So what are you, exactly?'

'Exactly? I'm not sure I know, exactly. A traveller, perhaps.'

'Like an alien?'

He looks puzzled, a touch dissatisfied by my lack of imagination.

'More earthly, I think.'

'Vampire?'

'Doubtful.'

'But I've only ever seen you when it's dark.'

'I have only let you see me when it is dark.'

I sigh. He seems to enjoy making it difficult. I would call him a ghost, yet he touched my hand, so has some kind of form.

'You might be the Devil for all I know.'

'Oh, the Devil has nothing on me.'

I'd laugh except I can tell he's not joking, so I continue to look at him with all the curiosity I can't pretend to hide. I'm looking to find a bit of the Devil in him, a line from crinkling his nose in a sneering way or a hardness to his eyes. In truth, there is nothing like that – perhaps the potential for it, but don't we all have that? He's surely a trickster of some kind, though: his wry playfulness carries an edge, one that could probably turn acerbic in the wrong circumstances.

I think of a way to test him.

'Name something that beats.'

'A strange request,' he muses. 'Something that beats? A heart?'

This makes me smile.

'You're not the Devil.'

'How do you surmise that from one enquiry?'

'Because someone cruel would look to something vicious that beats, a stick or a fist. People who are not cruel always say a heart. Music is also an acceptable answer, except people usually say music if they've heard the question before and want to sound clever.'

He thinks this over.

'How do you know that I have not heard the question before and said heart to sound kind?'

I chuckle at this because I don't have an answer. I already want to like him, this strange traveller, or whatever he might be. Whether he's living in my head or truly sitting here beside me, it's nice to have someone to talk to.

When I ask his name, he introduces himself as Bram.

'You're called Bram and you're *not* a vampire? But it's such a vampire name!'

This amuses him – a flicker of recognition, as if the idea isn't new.

'No. I am not a vampire. Vampires do not exist.'

'And you do?'

His tricksy smile deepens. He's not going to tell me much more about himself, and I have no idea whether this is down to him being evasive or my inability to ask the right questions.

'Was it you who moved the trolley out of the lift on Wednesday?'

He nods slowly, choosing his words with care. 'I wanted to know if you were paying attention.'

'And dropped the book in the basement?' I sound sterner at this.

'That was an accident.'

'An accident?'

'I was reading. You took me by surprise.'

'I took *you* by surprise?' If we were anywhere else, I would laugh out loud.

'People rarely see me.'

Does he mean rarely or never? Either way, I know the feeling.

For some reason, this makes me remember the silver origami star in my pocket, smaller even than the paper heart. They are so sweet and fragile that I don't want to lose either, so I fold them together into the shape of a heart that holds a star. They fit well.

'Why did you decide to talk to me?' I ask.

As I wait for his reply, I notice a young boy, no more than three or four years old, has crept up the stairs. He hovers at the edge of the recess, watching. Normally, I'm quick to spot children: they have a restless energy that fills a space. Somehow, he's snuck up on me.

Bram must share my sentiments as he has conveniently disappeared again.

I stand and give the boy a hard stare that I hope conveys my desire for him to keep his sticky hands off my sofa. Sadly, the minute I move away, he is climbing all over it.

5

Bram is leaning on the service desk when I let myself into the library later that evening. I didn't tell him I was coming back, but he is waiting as if it were an arrangement. When he smiles, his jewel eyes glint with a knowing curiosity.

I don't know if I trust him yet, but I'm too fascinated by his presence to entertain the alternative of hiding at home, watching TV.

When I say "arrangement", I don't mean a date. I haven't made a particular effort. I may have dug out my favourite emerald green jumper because it's about time I wore something more flattering, put on a bit of mascara and given my boots a long overdue buff, but I wouldn't want him to think I'm dressing to impress. Nevertheless, he seems pleased to see me as I come out of the shadows and into the ground floor's fierce spotlight.

'I would have thought this a strange place for a young person to frequent on a Saturday night,' he says. 'Are there no public houses or places to go dancing?'

'I'm not that kind of young person,' I reply. It's true. My Saturday nights are books or TV, like any other night. I would often read while The Black Eyed Boy killed zombies from the comfort of the sofa. Now, obviously, no more zombies.

'But you enjoy dancing.'

I shrug. 'What about you? Can you leave the library?'

'There are many places I can visit. A better question would be, can *you* leave the library?'

I frown. He must have seen me come in through the front door not one minute ago, and I can only arrive if I'd already left. The misgiving must be clear in my face as he flashes me another of his brilliant, knowing smiles. I shake my head, half-amused, and head for the front door.

'Not that way.'

He points in the opposite direction.

'But there's no door that way.'

Another brilliant smile. I follow him into the fiction section.

The darkness outside lets a sliver of moonlight peer through the stained glass of the tall window, enough for an orange glow to be reflected on the wall below. I look again, realising that it's not a reflection of the window but rather a door below it, slightly ajar so that the light from beyond radiates invitingly.

'After you,' Bram says. He holds out his hand, as he did for me to sit earlier. Almost too polite.

I hesitate. There is no door here: this is fiction (G-H). Yet I am looking perfectly clearly at a door. The orange glow is pulling me in, putting me in mind of warm spices baked into a cake or a bright hearth.

'Can you leave the library?' he asks again in his tricksy way.

Perhaps he is the Devil sending me through the door to Hell. Or perhaps he's bored of travelling alone. He could be both of those things.

I have a sense of waking, except I'm upright, standing in a field. It is night, and the breeze holds my hair as though I might be upside-down.

There is music, soft on the horizon. The grass is long and I realise as I walk that the music is coming not from further away, but from the steps I take here and now. I stop, the music quietens. I move to the left, the pitch sharpens. A skip to the right brings a key change. I laugh, and a silvery tinkle accompanies the melody, a triangle played lightly.

From a few metres ahead, Bram waves to me, his movement creating a further ripple of sound: woodwind, the scales of a clarinet. I hear my returned wave as a light piccolo.

'What is this place?'

My call is more like singing. It harmonises wonderfully with the vibration of Bram's swaying coat and fluttering hair as I approach him. He seems happy, a contented smile replacing the thoughtful curiosity that gave him a distant look in the library. I'd say it makes him look younger, but I have no idea how old he appears to be.

'This is Lyrium.'

He turns to walk alongside me. We are near a cliff edge, the grass dropping away a few steps to our left. It reminds me distantly of the village around the coast where my Aunt Bette lived. Instead of the sea sweeping beyond the cliff as it does in her village, there are the million warm lights of a city.

I try to say something like 'wow,' but it ends up a tuneful gurgle at the back of my throat.

'It reminds me of somewhere I know,' I tell him.

'That's the thing about the universe: everything is a little familiar.'

'How did we get here?'

'Through a door in the library.'

The library. That in itself barely seems real now.

'There are more doors?'

'Oh, many doors,' he sings. He sounds so pleased about it that his tone creeps up an octave. 'Many doors, many worlds.

Lyrium is but one.'

'And are they literal doors?'

He looks approving. 'Clever girl. I suppose you might consider them portals. I kept the analogy literal for your benefit.'

This sounds condescending, as if my poor little brain might not comprehend something so abstract as a portal that isn't a door.

'Oh. Thanks, I guess.' I reply with what I hope is the right level of sarcasm. 'Then are those *portals* open to anyone, or just to you?'

'Ah,' he says with a flourish. 'That, Flora Cotton, is the question!'

I have no idea what he means, but I can hear the music of the city now. It should be a cacophony, and yet it is smooth and harmonious. I'm listening to a world of bakers whose cinnamon bread sounds like a fiddler's reel; launderers whose soap bubbles rise and pop as a sweet operetta; grocers who call out in every language, every possible note.

So many notes. I stop and lean forward to catch my breath.

'Are you alright, Flora?' Bram places his hand on my shoulder. 'The vastness can be overwhelming.'

'I'm fine.'

I pull myself up and try not to wobble. The sensation of feeling music has made me seasick, but I don't want to miss anything.

'Would you like to go to the city?' he asks.

'Oh, I don't know…' I begin to say. It's getting late, and I've no idea how we're supposed to get home.

Without any warning, Bram grabs my hand and runs towards the cliff edge. I've got no choice but to run alongside him or I'll be dragged like a child's blanket through the musical grass. My protests come out in staccato bursts, and as we leap over the edge, I scream out an arc of musical notes visible all around me. We are held in the air – if I reach out, I could play the shiny notes as though they were piano keys.

Below, the lights of the city wink at us. My fear begins to shift. It's so beautiful, like the postcard my mum sent from Edinburgh. I'm filled with the notion that, if this is the last thing I ever see, at least I saw something magical before the end.

The thought is taking hold when we suddenly fall straight down. The real possibility of the end coming makes me shriek once more, a shimmering curve of crotchets and quavers swirling in our wake. We land on our feet in front of a newspaper kiosk.

'Good evening, sir,' Bram says to the vendor. 'How fares the world?'

'All quite well, sir,' the vendor replies, recovering quickly from the surprise of our arrival. His voice is a bassoon, rich and bassy.

'Excellent!'

Bram is now wearing a black stovepipe hat, which he raises to the vendor as we make our way along the street. I, too, have obtained a hat out of nowhere – a peaked beret in the same emerald green as my jumper, except this is no longer a jumper but a shirt that sits below a fitted black waistcoat. My loose cargo trousers have become tailored plus fours, and my calf-length boots are now cute, brogue-style ankle boots.

'What the…' I begin, trying to recover my senses. This can't be real. The city. These clothes. I don't understand. I look to Bram for answers, but he takes my arm as if we've done this a hundred times.

'Lyrium is our playground tonight,' he says expansively. 'What shall we do? Dine at the Wall of a Thousand Bells? Shop at the Midnight Boutique?'

I'm too dazed to respond, my mind racing to make sense of our surroundings. We take a cobbled lane of multicoloured houses criss-crossed with ornate beams, before turning into a piazza of cafés lined with tables and chairs, where people are enjoying an evening drink.

The harmony of their chatter is like a hundred orchestras all playing together. I can just make out the lights of a harbour in the distance, from which a breeze carries the driving, rhythmic beats of a shanty. It shouldn't work, it should all clash and fall out of time, yet it remains flawless.

We take a seat outside a café where Bram orders liqueurs and petit fours. He is comfortable here, as if he's visited many times. He doesn't stand out at all. I feel very provincial by comparison.

'I don't understand how any of this is happening,' I finally say.

'Must you understand?'

I scowl at him to show I'm serious. He just laughs, eyes twinkling.

'Can you at least tell me how I'm wearing different clothes here?'

'You don't like them?'

'Well, I mean, yes, I do.' I look down at the cute boots, which I have to admit are pretty fabulous. 'But that's not the point. Can you explain how I come to be wearing them?'

He gives me that knowing look again.

'Not on a scientific level, no.'

'How about on a not scientific level?' I persist.

He leans in. 'When you travel between worlds, you have the capacity to take other forms. It won't happen every time; it depends on the world. You usually end up taking the form that suits you at the time. This place clearly suits you.'

I can't help but blush.

When the petit fours arrive, they are shaped as musical notes and the plate on which they rest hums, a singing prayer bowl. I fiddle with one, sniffing the light fondant and holding it up to the moonlight before putting it in my mouth. It's like nothing I've ever tasted before, rich creaminess infused with sharp, fruity bursts that dance on my tongue.

It keeps me quiet for a while, and I begin to settle into the musical chatter around me, but my curiosity soon nudges restlessly back.

'So is there a door for every world, or can one door take you anywhere?'

'Flora,' Bram says, his tone firm. 'I know you are curious, but for tonight, could you please enjoy being in this great city and not worry so much?'

I consider this, taking another petit four and popping it into my mouth. A symphony.

'Okay.'

As we get up to leave the café, the wind catches Bram's hat. He has to hold it down. Something about this bothers him. He stands still for a minute, looking towards the harbour.

'Funny,' he says to himself.

'What's that?'

'Nothing?'

The way he says this as a question confuses me, as though he's seen someone he knows but can't quite be sure because they're out of place. He begins to walk towards an alleyway with a café on one corner and a bakery on the other. I follow tentatively.

'I don't think we should go down there,' I say. I may not

know Lyrium, but a dark alley is a dark alley anywhere, with all the grim possibilities that could entail.

'You can stay there if you like.'

Bram edges in and I'm compelled to follow, conscious that if something were to happen to him, I've got no idea how I'd get home. I stay within arm's reach of him as we nudge forward. I can't quite see ahead; there is only darkness.

He stops.

'What is it?' I whisper.

'What can you hear?'

'Nothing.'

'Exactly.'

I realise what he means. Lyrium is a place of sound and music, where you can hear all things all of the time. Here, there is silence. Silence that has never seemed so loud to me before.

'Flora, I need you to turn around very slowly. Whatever you do, don't touch anything.'

I turn without argument. Something new hovers in his tone – not fear exactly, but it makes me take him seriously enough to do what he says. The musical quality that has imbued his speech since we arrived has gone. We are talking normally.

'Now, when I say, I need you to run. Don't look back, just run.'

'What about you?'

'I'll be right behind you. Now, run!'

I move as quickly as I can, though something tugs at me, as if I'm being dragged under by a strong current. The square is ahead – I can see it – but no matter how fast I push forward, I'm stuck in place, moving without ever gaining ground. The lights begin to fade, dimming out, until there is only darkness: a night without stars.

I stumble, and the undulating cobbles dance towards me. I brace for the resonant clash of a cymbal hitting the ground. What comes is a dull thud as I skid across a stretch of carpet tiles and clatter into a shelving rack.

It takes me a minute to open my eyes. When I do, I'm lying on the floor in the moonlit library, surrounded by a pile of large-print historical romances that must have been dislodged by the force with which I hit the shelves. At first, I feel alone and disoriented. I can't remember how I came to be here. Then I remember the music. Lyrium. Bram.

'Bram?'

I see his eyes first, shining like a cat's eyes, before the rest of him takes shape. He is standing and looks comparatively unruffled.

'Are you alright?' he asks.

I'm distracted by my impulse to pull the fallen books together and reshelve them.

'Flora, are you hurt?'

'I don't think so.'

He holds out his hand to help me, and I try to lever myself up. A sharp pain shoots from my wrist to my elbow, making me sit back, wincing. I can feel a carpet burn on my knee, and there's a good chance I might throw up. Still, my wrist is the most pressing concern since I can't put any weight on it.

Bram bends to his knees and takes my wrist in his cold fingers.

'Let me see.'

'Why, are you a doctor?'

'Yes.'

'Oh.'

I watch him in silence. There's something about the way he holds me, the lightness of his touch, that makes me suppress a shiver. The only other man who has been this close to me is the one I thought I would spend the rest of my life with. Now he's gone, that entire life is gone, and there is this new man who may or may not be real, framed in starlight and looking back at me with eyes made of sapphires and emeralds and diamonds.

'It is not broken, merely a minor sprain.'

He helps me off the floor with my other hand. Something has lightened his spirits, though I'm not sure if it's knowing that I'm not badly injured or just the fact that we are back in the library.

'Well done, Flora,' he continues in a cheerful tone. 'I was not certain that you would be able to do that.'

I still don't have much capacity to speak. I'm tired and full of wonder, but also a little afraid. I'm not sure what happened there at the end, and that's the least of it. Then his words catch up. *I was not certain that you would be able to do that*. Do what?

'What do you mean?' I ask.

'Travel between worlds is dangerous. Not everyone can do it.'

I blink hard, trying to wrap my head around that.

'So when you asked if I could leave the library, it wasn't about whether I dared to leave, but whether I could physically make it through the door at all?'

'Of course. I have travelled extensively, but never with a human.'

His mood is bright now, while mine is darkening.

'I might have been in danger?'

'I hoped not, but what is life without a little risk?'

'I was, what, your canary down the mine?'

Naturally, I say this in an incredulous tone. I can feel the pinky blotch spreading across the top of my chest, which always happens when I'm nervous or angry. The pitch of my voice also heightens, so if he doesn't say something that rationalises all of this at once, I will become practically inaudible.

'Oh, canaries can travel between worlds without any problem at all. It is the more intelligent creatures that become problematic. The bat, for example, was another thing altogether.'

'Problematic?'

Practically inaudible.

'Creature?'

Actually inaudible.

6

I'm on the Coastrunner bus on my way to visit Aunt Bette, a bouquet of her favourite Arabian Night dahlias across my lap.

It's a Sunday, and if it were summer, the bus would be crowded with couples and families on day trips to the beach. As it's autumn, I get it mostly to myself. I've put a Tubigrip on my wrist, even though it feels a lot better this morning. There is also a faint medicinal smell from the antiseptic cream I've slathered on my knee.

It wasn't my intention to leave the library in a flounce last night, but being called a "problematic creature" made me too angry to argue the point with a man who was willing to take a gamble on my very existence. I went to bed in a huff, slept badly, and my dreams of music and dancing were plagued by wild canaries. They caught in my hair, throwing me off balance. I woke up realising I needed to talk to someone.

The bus passes through several rows of trees, and I gaze out into the alternate strips of dappled sunlight and shadow. There's a rational voice out there somewhere trying to tell me that technically Bram didn't call me a "problematic creature", but the inference pissed me off enough to leave him alone with a pile of large-print romances at his feet. I wonder now if he had the courtesy to shelve them. I picture that scene, and it's not without an element of humour. Then I start to fume again.

Honestly, it doesn't matter how real or materially ambiguous the men in my life are – they seem determined to ruin me.

Aunt Bette says I look well. I talk to her for a while about The Black Eyed Boy and 21 and Blonde and that whole saga. To be honest, I'm not as angry as I thought I would be when it all comes out.

'What would you be doing right now if you were still together?' she asks.

'Sunday afternoon. We'd be watching a film, probably spy action, and deciding what takeaway to have for dinner.'

'Sunday takeaway?'

'Every week!'

I've missed the sour face she pulls when she finds something distasteful.

'Didn't you used to enjoy having a roast dinner on a Sunday?'

'I did, but he didn't. He hates anything traditional.'

'Isn't a takeaway every Sunday a tradition?'

Aunt Bette always gets to the heart of things. She's like the smart heroines from the black and white movies she used to love: Rosalind Russell, Barbara Stanwyck, and of course, Bette Davis. I like to think of Aunt Bette spending her days playing cards with them in fancy hotel lounges, dressed in beaded gowns and drinking gin fizz all day long, classic blues playing in the background.

I end up telling her about Bram. I wasn't going to mention him – outside of the library, he is a daydream – but my thoughts tumble out.

'He's just so arrogant and secretive. I don't see what's wrong with wanting to understand things, but he seems to dismiss any curiosity as prying.'

'It's astonishing,' she sighs. 'You meet someone interesting, someone who takes your mind off what's been happening, shows you worlds you never knew existed – and you're complaining?'

This disturbs me, and I unwrap the dahlias, carefully pushing each thick stem into the holes of the grave vase so that they stand up straight.

'I could have died, you know.'

I hope she'll laugh, enjoy the irony.

'Quatsch!' she cries. 'Besides, you can die crossing the road. I ought to know.'

'But it would be my choice to weigh the risks and take my chances knowing the potential outcomes.'

'That's true. But sometimes you'll find yourself head-on with something bigger and faster than you, whether you made a choice or not.'

'I suppose so,' I concede.

'Have you talked to your mum about it? I'm sure she'd understand.'

I shake my head. It's too fanciful a thing even for my quixotic mother to make sense of. Besides, I don't want to talk about her. I must look quite disagreeable as Aunt Bette tilts her head, gives me that searching look they both share.

'You want her to be happy, don't you, Flora?'

'Of course. I just didn't think that meant moving to the other end of the country and dating a werewolf!'

'A werewolf, indeed!' Aunt Bette scoffs. 'You're still prone to such fancies.'

She takes a final drag through her cigarette holder, long nails clenched like tiger claws. I miss her terribly.

'Your new friend was rash, but at least he wanted to share something brilliant with you.'

I nod, thoughtful.

'I wonder why?'

She falls quiet too, starts to fade. It's a good question.

That's the thing about the universe: everything is a little familiar.

I'm considering Bram's words from the clifftop that I'd thought of as I wandered through the enchanted grass of Lyrium. It's not as I remember it from childhood visits. The edge is fenced off with a wire net that's caught every discarded wrapper blown out from the arcade of takeaway stands behind me. The grass is sallow and patchy, speckled with dog shit.

In my childhood memories, this place was a windswept panorama haunted by the romance of the sea. There is little romance here now, only the sad rustle of empty packets trying to escape their wiry prison.

What Aunt Bette said has merit, and my thoughts turn to this as I watch two gulls wrestle with the scraps of last night's fish and chips.

I did meet someone interesting, and for those few hours, The Black Eyed Boy didn't cross my mind once.

7

It's dark when I get back to town, and I go straight to the library. Bram is upstairs on the sofa, reading my copy of *The Count of Monte Cristo*. He must have heard me making my way up the stairs, but he doesn't look up.

'So, can you leave the library through the front door?' I ask him.

He glances over the top of the book.

'I have not tried. This world holds risks for me. I am not sure.'

'Then how about we find out?'

Bram closes the book and sets it on the sofa. His clothes are different: he is wearing a more modern tailored jacket over a high-necked jumper in some sort of inky midnight shade. He looks good.

'Would you not prefer to discover a new door with me? See where else we might go?'

He must know I would, but I've become curious about how much of my world Bram can be exposed to, whether he could even exist out there.

'Surely it's only fair for you to do something new yourself. If you're willing to risk my existence, maybe you should show me that you're also willing to risk your own.'

He walks towards me. I keep forgetting how tall he is.

'Flora, please forgive me,' he says. 'Last night, I should have been more cautious.'

His apology catches me off guard. It sounds sincere, which I'm not used to. When The Black Eyed Boy left, he said, "I'm sorry," but he may as well have been saying "see ya" or "have a good one" for all the emotion he conveyed. This is different. It has weight.

'It's okay,' I reply, reaching out to take his hands. It's the first time I've done this. I've let him come close enough to touch me, but this is different. I'm not just telling him that I forgive him. I'm trying to say that we are linked now – friends, or something like that. There's so much I still don't know about him and the worlds he travels. I want the chance to find out.

'The front door, then!' he says, as if daring it to lead somewhere.

We descend the stairs together, and the gentle accord between us grows good-humoured, becoming a wry kind of bravado when we reach the front door, as if daring each other to be the first to back out. I watch as Bram reaches for the handle.

'Wait!' I breathe, hesitating, the fear of being alone tightening around me. If he's never stepped outside before, would he simply vanish? Is he willing to risk that? Am I? Perhaps he predicted this and is playing a game, getting as close as he dares. Or maybe he really is willing to put himself in danger so that I'll trust him.

'Now or never, Flora.'

'Let's go somewhere else,' I say. I want to sound impulsive rather than afraid, but I'm probably not all that convincing.

'Head to the basement stairs and look to your left.'

I start to walk that way when another thought occurs to me.

'One thing before we go, how many others have there been?'

'Others?'

Heat rises to my cheeks. That sounded more loaded than I meant it to. I'm trying to picture the pattern – who else has he taken on these strange journeys, and what became of them?

'After the canaries and the… bat, was it?'

'Since the bat? None from this world. Until you, that is.'

'So why me?'

'Excuse me?'

Does he really not get it? It seems plain enough.

'I'm curious about why you… What you…' I fumble, wary that it sounds like self-doubt. 'Why me?' I repeat, a little flustered.

'Why not you?'

Surely he's being tricksy again.

'It's a reasonable question.'

'And a reasonable answer. I am not sure what else to say. You because you were there. You because you haunt this place as I do.'

'But I'm not a ghost.'

He looks back at me with an *are you sure* sort of look, but stops short of saying it.

'Come on! Do you want to argue, or do you want an adventure?'

He takes my hand, leads me back through the spotlight. Sure enough, the wall beside the stairwell sits partially open, a mysterious red glow beckoning us to the other side.

The light is red because the sky beyond the door is red. Not quite blood red, but there is drama to our surroundings.

We are on a path leading up a craggy hill, lined with trees that have been bent and gnarled by the wind so they appear to be reaching out to us in supplication. I can make out what must be a ruin in the distance, circled by hundreds of birds. Everything is silhouetted by the ruby sky.

Bram looks around to get his bearings. He seems approving.

'Magda,' he says warmly as I try to keep pace beside him.

'This place is called Magda?'

'Magda is not a place,' he chuckles.

'Right.' I don't get it. 'So where are we?'

'This is the realm of the Bat Queen. That building is her castle.'

I look ahead and realise that they are not birds hovering around the building. They are bats. There's a darting, erratic speed to their motion.

'You know her, this Bat Queen?'

'Oh yes, we go back a long way.'

'And will she mind us turning up?'

He has to think about this, which makes me nervous.

'Just be fearless, the version of yourself that is not afraid of anything. You'll get on perfectly well. Oh, and take this.'

He pulls something from his pocket and places it in my palm. At first, I think it's a kidney bean. On closer inspection, I see that it shimmers in an oil slick of blues and greens. I'm horrified.

'Is that a dead bluebottle?'

'Of course. Would you visit royalty without taking a gift?'

It's ridiculous, but I can't argue, even though the clammy feel of the dead fly in my palm makes my skin crawl. I put it in my pocket and wipe my hand down the leg of my trousers.

As we come closer to the castle, I can hear music. Not a tuneful melody, more of a meditative composition, like whale song. Closer still, and there is no door but an open archway of solid stone. From inside, I can hear a woman's voice. She doesn't sound happy.

'...and when you've finished, make sure that bloody spider can't get back in!'

'Maybe I should wait here,' I whisper to Bram.

'Don't be silly.'

Bram takes the lead through the arch, and I scuttle in behind him. My eyes are slow to adjust to the gloom inside. I can make out two tall figures standing ahead of us. One takes a long bow to the other before turning and heading through a further archway beyond. There's a flapping, rustling sound as they leave.

The figure that remains must be the woman whose voice I heard. I can see her clearly now. She wears a long black dress, fitted around her hips and legs but flaring into a wide hem that ripples out over the flagstone floor like spilt paint. The dress collar is high, and brushes against a fine line of greyish-brown down that runs up her pointed cheekbones and into a strip of longer hair on her head. She looks at us with jet black eyes, and I'm so terrified that I can't help taking a step towards Bram.

'Well, isn't this perfect?' she snaps through sharp little teeth. 'The hunt flies have escaped, *all* of my cousins have turned up, and now – humans!'

Bram appears oblivious to her mood and holds out his hands to her, planting a kiss on the side of her face.

'My dearest Magda.'

'Abraham,' she replies testily, though she takes his kiss with grace. Then she looks at me and I hold my breath. Those eyes: I see nothing in them, yet they must see everything.

'Have we interrupted something?' Bram asks.

'Only my granddaughter's wedding.'

Magda's eyes stay fixed on me as she speaks, and I feel a total fool for being unable to follow Bram's advice about how to behave. I'm a textbook example of the freeze response.

'This is my friend, Flora Cotton.'

Fear is trying to bubble up my windpipe and spread out to my arms. I manage to put my hand in my pocket and pull out the dead bluebottle.

'I bring a gift, your majesty,' I say. My hand shakes, but at least I don't drop the fly.

Magda's gaze turns momentarily from my face to my palm as she unfurls long fingers, black nails curling back around her fingertips. She takes the fly and places it in her mouth, chews exquisitely, as though it were a luxurious truffle.

'Thank you, Flora Cotton.' She gives me one final, thoughtful look before turning back to Bram. 'At least your guest has some manners, Abraham. I suppose you'll have to stay for the reception now. It would be rude for me to send you away and even ruder for you to leave. You've missed the ceremony, though, and I doubt you'll want to join the hunt.'

'Most kindly, your majesty.' Bram bows practically to the floor.

'I'll make your accommodations suitable for humans.'

I assume this means that she's going to call out to someone to make arrangements for us, but the room shifts, mirage-like, and where a moment ago there was stone, there are now plush red carpets, gilded stucco walls and huge chandeliers dripping from the high ceiling.

'Is this acceptable?' she asks. I realise she is looking at me, not Bram.

'Er, yes,' I say. 'Th… thank you, your majesty.'

She says nothing more, just sashays away through the back arch.

The room is not the only thing that has changed. I appear to be wearing a gown, black metallic satin with a floor-length pleated skirt and a neckline that comes right off my shoulders. There's a platinum chain around my neck from which a bat-shaped pendant hangs, encrusted with diamonds, and my hair is curled into ringlets that fall to my collarbone. I've never dressed like this before in my life. Seeing my bare shoulders makes me feel completely naked.

'Oh my GOD!'

I twist around in a failed attempt to cover myself with my arms, realising as I move that there are silver sandals on my feet with thin, high heels, jewelled straps snaking up my ankles. 'I can't wear this!'

'Of course you can.'

Bram is wearing a morning suit, a silvery waistcoat embroidered with the black lines of bat wings. I shouldn't keep protesting, but he has gotten off lightly by comparison.

'I can't walk in these shoes!'

'Then please allow me to escort you.'

He holds out his arm, and I take it with a nervous sigh – mostly for balance, although it seems to be the right thing to do. I must look like a clockwork doll as I walk, because I'm so unused to heels. The last time I wore any kind of heel was at a colleague's wedding during my factory days. That was more of an adorable kitten heel, not these vicious spikes.

'You look beautiful,' Bram says.

Now I definitely need something to cover my neck: the pink flush is pouring out over my chest again.

'So do you,' I reply. I mean it, too. The way the sharp lines of the suit echo the angles of his face. It's almost too perfect. I have to look away or I'll turn from pink to scarlet.

As we pass through the second archway, the reception is in full swing. There are bat-people with the same humanoid features as Magda, as well as tiny pipistrelles flapping around and all sorts of species in between. I've never seen anything like it, even in storybooks, and make a special effort not to gawp.

'Lord Abraham and Lady Flora Cotton of the Human Realm.'

We are at the top of a short flight of stairs as a humanoid attendant announces us. Only a few of the guests take any notice before returning to their chatter.

Looking closer, there are others here who are not bats, though we are few. A duck-man holding a coupe glass of champagne laughs in a vibrant quack along with a fruit bat hanging from a chandelier, while what looks like a floating bedsheet pauses to firm itself around a tray of wriggling canapés.

There are so many amazing things to look at: giant ice sculptures shaped as bats in various poses; tables topped with intricate candelabra; and, at the far end of the room, dancing that looks more like aerobatics – bats and bat-people spinning in dizzying, airborne reels.

Magda looks very regal as she circulates among her guests, and that must be her granddaughter with her in a long gown of black chiffon. She is a young version of Magda, with the same black eyes and sharp features.

I descend the stairs without falling and begin scanning the room for somewhere to sit so that I can get out of these ridiculous shoes.

'We should dance!' Bram announces.

'Not a chance!' I reply.

'Nonsense. Parties are for dancing, and I know you love to dance.'

I look at him with a tight expression. I suppose I do enjoy the music, a sort of pulsating quiver of sound that I can feel rather than hear, and I am meant to be playing the version of myself that is not afraid of anything. But still.

'What if I fall?'

'You won't.'

'I might.' It's a mumbled retort, and he smiles, knowing he's won already.

'Trust me, Flora. I won't let anything bad happen.'

It begins as a waltz. There is space on the floor for us, and we join in a fluid, seamless motion. I can hear the light fluttering of gowns and rested wings waiting to open.

It's nice to move; I enjoy the freedom, the fluidity, and the feeling of Bram's hand on my back. I become aware of my body, of being here and now, and notice, at the same time, that the floor is no longer beneath me: we've taken flight!

I shift, not quite panicking, but a slight pause in our motion threatens to throw me backwards. Bram still has hold of me and pulls me closer.

'Don't look down,' he whispers.

As we shift back into the cycle, it's as if we're floating on a current: a ribbon caught in the breeze. I'm moving in rhythm with the shapes around me, flashes of flapping fabric that whirl and loop like torn sails whipping past my body, my face. We dive between them, and I may be a bat or I may be a human; I can't tell any more.

I spin and laugh, and there's Bram, and we pull each other up and up, faster and faster, in featherless flight. I'm not going to fall. I'm not going to break. I am here. I am there. Light as air.

When the dance ends, I'm a mixture of things. Elated. Ecstatic. Exhausted. I struggle to catch my breath, and being back on the ground feels odd.

'Let me get you a drink,' Bram says, leaving me to wait beside an ice sculpture of a bat in full flight. I steady myself against the sculpture, my feet aching. I need to sit down, but instead watch Bram heading towards a silver fountain pouring out red wine. At least I hope it's wine.

'Are you enjoying the party, Flora Cotton?'

Magda is beside me as though she simply appeared. She indicates a velvet chaise, reading my mind.

'Yes, thank you. And please, call me Flora.'

'Flora. Such a pretty name.'

She's not hostile, but there is a tangible sense of tension as she sits alongside me, as if I'm Eve Harrington in *All About Eve* and about to be given advice that is actually a thinly veiled warning, not the role I anticipated playing tonight.

'Tell me about yourself, Flora.'

'Er…' I falter. I have all the scope in the world to say whatever fanciful thing I choose, and my brain has seized up as if I'm at a job interview.

'How about your family?' Magda says in a parody of helpfulness.

'Family?'

'Parents? Siblings?'

'Well, my dad died when I was little. I can't remember much about him, just an outline really. He had a beard, but I only know that from photos. He was ill for a long time.'

That's more detail than I thought I'd share. Am I rambling now because I'm nervous, or does she have some power to draw out the truth? Either way, I can't fathom why someone so captivating would be interested in anything as ordinary as my life.

'And your mother?'

'She lives in Edinburgh. She's dating a werewolf.'

'A werewolf? I didn't realise the Human Realm had werewolves.'

'He's not really a werewolf. He's a Civil Engineer called Cyril.'

As I say it, I appreciate how funny it sounds in the context of where I sit now: this fantastical backdrop surely far more accommodating of an actual werewolf. Cyril isn't a particularly werewolfish name, but my mum sent me a photo not long after they got together and he has wild hair that flips out at the sides and eyes that look as though they could get caught up in the moon, so the visual is pure lycan – an odd pairing with my sunshine mum in her bright, floaty dress.

'I've started to wonder if I only know her by memory now, too. She's adventurous and funny, thinks I should be more supportive of her choices, but that it's fine to chip away at mine. We don't talk much.'

'That's a shame. It is a tragedy when families become divided. No siblings?'

'No. I had an aunt, but…' I trail off to silence, feeling even more tragic. It hasn't occurred to me until now quite how solitary my life has become.

'And how long have you known Abraham?'

I have to think about it. Firstly, I just can't think of him as an Abraham, though I am aware that Bram is a shortened version of the name. Secondly, the time seems immaterial.

'Two days,' I reply. 'That is, two Earth days.'

I realise too late how stupid that sounds.

'I know what you meant. I am from your world originally, after all. I came here with Abraham many years ago.'

She enjoys my surprise, and I remember something Bram said when we returned from Lyrium: *The bat was another thing altogether*. Magda must be the bat he was alluding to, though I had assumed from the way he talked that the poor thing met a messy end in passing between realms. It didn't occur to me that he might have meant an ordinary animal transforming into anthropomorphic royalty. Why would it?

'Are you falling in love with him?'

Another question, another surprise. This time, I hold my nerve. I cling to the version of myself in flight, the one who isn't afraid. What would she say, that confident woman in the black ball gown, diamonds at her throat?

'I find him interesting. Very charming. But that's not the same as love.'

'A good answer,' Magda approves. 'Non-committal, of course, though it was rather an impolite question. Abraham is a wonderful man, but he can be fickle. You'll learn that – I hope at not too great a cost.'

There it is, the warning. It clarifies so much: the way she speaks to me, the way she behaves with Bram, the reluctant fondness she carries for him. It's different from that of a platonic friend.

'You were lovers.'

It's not a question. I expect an offhand response. Instead, the notion seems to make her wistful. She leans back in her seat, the spectacle of dancing and revelry catching a reflection of the past she stares into.

'I came here with him from your realm, built this place. Our time together was brief. Seeing him reminds me of the mess time makes of us all, even here. There are very few of our descendants left.'

'Descendants? You had children?'

She nods, gazing out into her misty remembrances.

'Our daughter, Ralina. She's long gone now, as are most of my children. This realm is immortal, but bats are sensible and rarely crave immortality. It's a dangerous thing. Most return to your realm or find other mortal places.'

I can picture long-gone Ralina, a sweet little bat with jewel eyes and sharp teeth. I look at Magda and consider how an immortal mother can stand the loss of her mortal children. Then I imagine my own mother sharing the same burden, and I can feel their despair, how much it must hurt them.

'I'm sorry,' is all I can say.

A shadow passes in front of us. It's Bram, holding a glass of wine out to each of us. I take one, but Magda stands and bids him to sit with me.

'The hunt will begin soon. I need to find the box of gadflies gifted from the Magpie King, or it will look bad. Do say goodbye before you leave this time, Abraham.'

Bram kisses Magda's hand with a grand flourish, and she rolls her dark eyes as she walks away. He settles into her seat with a conspiratorial look.

'What were the two of you talking about?'

My impulse is to say we were talking about love, about the passage of time, about his daughter and her descendants, the pain of both mortality and immortality. It's too big.

'She told me you were lovers.' I keep my tone light, relaxed. 'That you had a daughter.'

'It was a long time ago,' he says.

'Really, you don't have to explain.'

'As you know, any form may change across the realms, and I was taking the form of a bat at the time, so it is not as strange as it may sound.'

I sniff my glass, relieved that it smells like actual wine, and take in my surroundings. I'm not sure why he needs to explain this. Magda is a bat, but she is also a woman. Of all the things I might appreciate an explanation for, the complications of sex are not among them.

'Bram, it doesn't sound strange at all.'

We can tell it's time to leave because the bats are getting restless. There's a hunger in their eyes. It's time for the hunt, and I'm glad not to be on the menu.

As we come back to the archway at the front of the castle, everything has returned to stone, and our party clothes are gone. I'm a little sad about this; I was beginning to enjoy swanning around in a ball gown. Surprisingly, the jewellery around my neck remains, the bat-shaped pendant glinting as Magda arrives to bid us farewell. It is less elaborate now, more akin to the sort of silver jewellery I would normally wear – the centre of the pendant has settled into the form of a small solitary diamond.

Bram gives the Bat Queen another of his deep bows. It is so exaggerated that there must be some sort of irony to it, a long-held joke between them. Do we always grow fond of our old lovers in the end, when the dust settles and those old pains are replaced by new ones?

'Don't leave it so long next time,' she tells him. 'We must talk about The Chattering soon.'

'Of course, your majesty.'

'And Flora, the necklace is my gift to you. For protection.'

I go to thank her, but she pulls me in for a cosmopolitan air kiss, whispering in my ear.

'Try not to fall too hard.'

'I'll try,' I reply, though we both know it might be too late.

PART TWO
BITTER FRUIT

8

My terraced house has a small yard at the back that catches the sun in the morning. It's nothing much – a few potted herbs, hardy ones like rosemary and lavender, and a wooden bistro set that squeals whenever it's moved. I wanted to get the wire one I saw in the garden centre, sage green with painted daisies twisting up the legs and around the edge of the tabletop. The Black Eyed Boy opted for this one on account of it being a third of the price. I imagined we would sit here together on Sunday mornings, drinking coffee and reading the papers. I didn't win that battle either.

It's unexpectedly warm and sunny this morning, so I'm sitting outside having my breakfast, turning the bat pendant of my necklace around in my fingers and mulling over the events of last night. My coffee has gone cold.

By the time we left the Bat Realm, I had warmed to Magda. It would be presumptuous to say that we became friends, but there was a definite spark of understanding there. I suppose that's how friendship begins, in those small glimmers of connection that can catch you by surprise.

And what of Bram? I'm not sure, he's such a mystery, and I still don't understand his interest in me. What was it he said last night? *You haunt this place as I do.* Does he pity me? Or does he make a habit of whisking young women away?

For all I know, he could have Flora Cottons scattered across a multitude of worlds.

Should I be more afraid of him? Probably, but there's something about him that is simultaneously terrifying and reassuring. I can't explain it.

Try not to fall too hard.

Magda's words swoop and dive in the morning ether. I can't catch them. When I try, they shift into an image of me physically falling, landing with a thud as I clatter into a shelf full of books, which isn't what she meant. It makes sense, yet it doesn't. How can I fall for a man if I don't know who he is?

When I met The Black Eyed Boy, I thought I was in love. Passing him in the canteen made my heart flutter because I caught him looking at me, and I wasn't used to male attention. He had a relaxed, effortless way about him. I couldn't believe it when he spoke to me. I was shy and barely said a word on our first date, but he didn't seem to mind. His favourite things were watching TV and playing video games, which suited me – there was no pressure to be interesting, no expectation that I'd dazzle him with conversation. I thought that comfort had depth, a kind of intimacy. But does all of that add up to love? The ease, the quiet, the lack of expectation? It certainly wasn't love that made him sleep with someone else, not while he was living in my house.

And now, with Bram, I have no idea what to think. I feel like a different person around him, one that's lighter, more playful, as if I'm discovering parts of myself I didn't know were there. But then I wonder: am I trying so hard to avoid the old patterns that I've ended up swinging in the opposite direction? Am I overcompensating, trying to be someone I'm not to avoid the mistakes of the past?

My thoughts are getting muddled. I shake my head, check my phone. There's a message from my mum, a photo of her standing at the top of a sculpted spiral staircase. She's captured the swirling curves of the balustrade so that it resembles a giant eye peering up behind her as she grins at the camera, thumbs-up. The picture says *look at all the great stuff you'd see if you were here*!

I let out a snorted almost-laugh at how deliberately ridiculous and touristy she looks. She's always been excited by variety, seeing new things.

'One day, when your dad's better, we'll go all over the world together,' she would say when I was a little girl, as we sat at Dad's bedside poring over pictures in old travel magazines. 'We'll go to The Parthenon and The Colosseum and Uluru and Machu Picchu and Marrakech. It'll be amazing!'

But Dad never got better. The amazing plans became a series of jobs to pay the mortgage. Raising a kid on her own. Then Edinburgh. Then the werewolf.

I should be happy for her. I know I should.

The library is busy all afternoon. There's a toddler group in for the first hour, from which I manage to keep a suitable distance, followed by a clear-up of the related carnage. At closing, I have to practically drag a couple of young teenagers away from the computers.

Once everyone else is gone, I find Bram sitting at a table by the front door where we pile up returned books. There's a small window that overlooks the park, and he is taking in the darkening world.

I stand beside him to see what he sees: the tattooed guy who works in the café across the road bringing in the A-board, turning out the lights; commuters filing through the luminescence of the streetlights at the edge of the park;

cars snaking their way along roads too narrow for them, designed many years ago with carriages in mind.

'Motor cars,' he says when he notices me beside him. 'Quite astonishing.'

I watch him thinking. I've decided I like looking at him. He has a beauty that is almost chilling, spectral, and yet at the same time makes my fingertips tingle at the idea of touching. Perhaps I like that he is an enigma, and it is this that makes him beautiful. Do I really need to know more? Of course I do, my curiosity in him is overwhelming.

'You don't have cars where you come from?'

'Only after a fashion.'

'You've never told me where that is,' I say. Subtle but definite. Well, I thought it was definite. He avoids it, eyes cast out towards the park as though in contemplation – one I can't penetrate. But I'm sure he heard me.

'I sit here in the morning sometimes. Look out at the park. Listen to the birds. Do you like the park, Flora?'

'Yes.'

'It must be nice.'

'So you've never been out into this world?'

He finds this amusing. 'Have you?'

I baulk at his tricksiness, always flipping things back. 'I walk to work and back every day for a start!'

'Work and back!' He shakes his head as though I'm the one being tricksy now. 'What of the rest of the world? I've seen you looking at books about India and Africa. The Americas. Have you seen them for yourself?'

It's true, I've never been abroad, unless you count a waterlogged campsite in Wales last year. The Black Eyed Boy spent the whole weekend trying to find Wi-Fi.

'No.'

'Don't you have family you could visit?'

'How about some music?' I say to change the subject, because I can do that too.

Bram is fascinated with the audio section, but doesn't know much about music in this world. I play a variety of songs through the speaker to see what he likes. He finds modern rock a bit raucous, modern pop a bit insipid, but he likes the classic rock, particularly the 60s blues and prog variety. Cal would be pleased.

We play The Moody Blues' *Days of Future Passed,* and when *Nights in White Satin* comes on, he bids me to stand.

'It's a waltz,' he says, taking my hand in his, holding me around the waist. We spin circles through the winding maze of fiction, each drum beat marking the soft pattern of my heart. I was never a fan of the song: I found it cheesy. *Beauty I'd always missed, with these eyes before.* Now I could listen to it on repeat.

I can't speak. Not the way I used to.

A rush of air tumbles through me, cool and exhilarating. For a moment, I think I'm diving into a vast pool of water, but when I try to turn, I realise something trails behind me, weightless and billowing. I am vapour. Something new. I have no bones, no skin. I have no form at all.

Beside me, another current of vapour streams through the air. It is Bram. He, too, is transformed, a ribbon of silvery cloud threaded with light. Where I glow with a soft, verdant luminosity, like phosphorescence under the sea, he shines in hues of opalescent grey, shifting as he moves.

'Flora, come this way!'

These are not words as I would normally understand them, but this is what he has said. They arrive as a feeling, a shimmering sequence of chimes or something like Morse code. And yet I understand him perfectly.

Above and below us, the sky is ablaze with stars. No, not just stars, but massive, looming planets, close enough to see the folds and storms of their atmospheres. Constellations twist in unfamiliar patterns, and galaxies spiral like distant fireworks.

'Where are we?' I ask, or think I ask. The words feel more like vibrations.

A door must have led us here. I can't remember. For once, I don't even care how this happened. I simply twist in a slow somersault, giddy with the freedom of it all, the motion smooth and unimpeded by gravity.

'The edges of the universe are full of dimensions such as these.'

I hear Bram's reply as a delighted chime, a note of pleasure that rings through the ether like he is pleased to see me so happy. So free. He flits to my side, a streak of light beside my green glow, and I feel his presence as an echo of warmth. We circle one another, drifting and darting, an effortless dance. I think this might be the most perfect moment of my entire life.

'Race you to the nearest planet!' I cry, surging ahead, leaving a glittering trail behind me like the tail of a comet. I feel untouchable – reckless, radiant, unstoppable.

Up ahead, a giant planet hangs, bathed in golden light from a distant sun. Its surface swirls with cloud patterns and molten seas, ringed with halos of debris and light. Twin stars burn beyond it in whitish-blue brilliance, pale and piercing. I hurtle towards it, drunk on momentum and joy. I feel as though I could reach it first, pierce its atmosphere and tumble laughing through its storms.

Something shifts.

A blur, dark and formless, rises in the space between me and the planet. It doesn't move like me or Bram. It doesn't drift or dance. It lurks, like gathering smoke.

A jolt of dread ripples through me. In a flash of motion, Bram darts ahead, his vapour twisting into a protective spiral.

'This way, Flora!' His tone peals urgently.

We twist together, diving, darting away from the blur. The joy has drained away: in its place is the chill of pursuit. I try to glance back, to see what it is. There is only a smear of darkness. Whatever it is, it's behind us. Gaining.

'Lower!' Bram calls. 'We need to get back to the door!'

I follow him, and the space below us ripples. I catch a glimmer, like a reflection on water, a tear in the fabric of this place. A doorway?

Still the presence follows. I push harder, diving low, the stars above growing distant. My form pulses with urgency. Whatever that thing is, it means to take something I'm not ready to give.

The ripples tighten, no longer soft distortions but a sudden pull, a vacuum drawing space inward, folding it like paper. I can't tell if I'm being swallowed or unravelled. I scream – sharp and instinctive, convinced the dark thing has caught me, that it's dragging me into itself.

The sensation shifts. I'm not being pulled apart. I'm being pulled through.

Something solid takes hold of me as the world snaps back into gravity and weight and form. It's Bram, his arms wrapped tight around me as we tumble, crash-landing in a heap on the floor of the library below the shining spotlight.

Neither of us speaks. We're just breathing. His embrace is firm and real, and I feel a new sort of feeling. Partly fear and partly something else.

'Flora?' he whispers, voice edged with concern. 'Are you alright?'

'I'm okay,' I murmur. I should probably move – steady myself, check I'm actually in one piece. But I don't. I don't want to break this moment, this closeness.

'Something was chasing us,' I say, still only half grounded. 'What was it?'

He hesitates.

'Nothing that should concern you.'

I look at him, his face so close to mine. His eyes flick away, just for a second, enough to shift the mood. His arms release me.

'Perhaps those distant dimensions are a little too dangerous,' he says, helping me to stand. He straightens quickly, as if putting some space between us.

'I'm not a child, Bram.'

He gives me such an inscrutable look in reply that I honestly don't know what to say.

9

A new door, a new world. Sparkling heat dances across my face as we move out of fleeting shadow into full sunshine. The air is dry, and a wave of sound hits me: not the resonant melodies of Lyrium, but a rushing soundscape of busy motion.

'The Market of Pam Angra,' Bram says.

We are quickly consumed by the bustle of a marketplace unlike any I have seen before, rows of huge stalls piled high with colourful spices and strange-looking vegetables, busy people making their way in every direction.

I find it hard to take it all in, and I'm cautious as I follow Bram. My initial instinct is to cover my ears against the noise: the shouting of vendors, the chatter and footfall, the ambient sounds of trade. I get a sense of a collective bustling around me, and that my presence disrupts the usual order. A couple of times, I bump arms or elbows with passers-by and automatically apologise, dodging merchants whose sales technique involves waving everything from long strings of beads to a live chicken right in my face.

The people here are mostly tall humanoids, with thin, ovoid faces and uncannily large eyes that peer at me from below the hoods of flowing robes in every possible colour. I am also wearing robes, forest green, and they are heavy, but I enjoy the protection, a shield against the exuberant energy of this place. Bram's are the colour of slate.

'We are on the main street here,' Bram calls over the noise as I try to keep up with his long strides, sidestepping another faceful of feathers. It is too much to take in at once and my senses are jumbled, as if I can taste the citrus of the bright robes on my tongue, hear the shrieking pots of cumin and turmeric.

The language of the vendors is a series of throaty, glottal sounds accompanied by wild hand gestures. It's very forceful and expressive, unsettling to a stranger like me who spends her days in a library.

Bram must sense my discomfort, leading us along a quieter row of busy seamstresses and lacemakers. Their nimble work is more soothing, concentration never wavering. Another, narrower row, and we are among the potters, the earthy tones of their materials grounding me as much as the quiet attentiveness of their making. Another corner and we come to a row of booksellers.

I linger to peruse some of the volumes without recognising the alphabet: strings of symbols or hieroglyphs. I can breathe easier with fewer bodies fighting for space.

'I'd forgotten how busy it gets,' Bram says, watching me take in the symbols on the covers of the books, all beautiful hardbacks.

'Is there something in particular you want?' I ask him.

'Hmm?'

His brow lifts a fraction, like he's not sure if I'm talking about books or something else.

'I mean, from the market.'

'Oh. No. I thought it would make a change for you, that is all.'

He's right, the busy pace is very different to that of my home town. I feel happy here, with him, among the books.

I want to pick them up, flick through the pages, penetrate these alien alphabets describing whole new worlds I can barely scratch the surface of. I don't have the nerve, so I just smile at the vendor who gives me a polite nod, the opposite of the pushy exuberance a few streets away.

'Amazing,' I say. It doesn't feel like enough.

We stroll further, past a stall of etched stones and carved wooden slats, their surfaces glowing amber in the bright sunlight. It is almost peaceful here, at the furthest edge where the stone of the marketplace meets the sand of the desert. To my left, there are fabric stalls dense with racks of coloured silks and gauzes that flutter like butterfly wings, revealing fleeting glimpses of their delicate patterns. To my right, clusters of houses wend across the sand, their sun-bleached façades catching the sunlight in a mosaic of muted pastels.

We pass through the dancing fabrics towards a small stand selling one type of fruit, round and pink. I watch Bram procure one from within the wave of white sheets that surround the stall, billowing around me like I'm standing in clouds.

Soft music begins to drift out across the market, a flute and a light drum. I remember our waltz, then that moment we crashed back into the library, Bram holding me tight. My gaze falls away when I see him looking back.

When he returns, he hands me a segment of fruit.

'Is that grapefruit?' I ask. My tone is wary. It appears that some horrors will persist everywhere in the universe. 'I hate grapefruit.'

'Try it. It's very refreshing.'

I can't help feeling a flicker of resentment at how easily he talks me into things, like now, when I put a segment of fruit in my mouth and instantly wish I hadn't. I may be light years from home, but grapefruit is still grapefruit in the same way as a dark alley is still a dark alley, wherever you may be. I try to keep it all at the front of my mouth, hiding the bitter pith in my teeth. My eyes water as the astringent juice hits my taste buds.

'How is it?'

'It's really bad,' I say through gritted teeth. My eyes are stinging now. I expect Bram to make some comment about me not trying hard enough. To my surprise, he laughs. It's so unexpected that I laugh too.

'Why is that funny?' I ask, even though I'm also laughing. I can't remember the last time I laughed for no good reason. I watch as laughter lines stretch across his face, and it's infectious – the laughter riding its course from him to me and back again. Vendors are looking at us curiously. A woman passing with a dawdling child pulls the little one out of our way, as if the contagion may spread.

As we walk on, I'm still chuckling. Bram keeps eating, though he knows better than to offer me any more grapefruit.

We stray away from the market, heading into narrow streets where washing dries high above our heads between tall, whitewashed buildings. There is noise and chatter, but it's more of a burble, like the white noise of a TV in the next room. I watch a skinny dog chase an even skinnier cat out of a shady alleyway, hitting the wall as the cat scrambles to a second-floor ledge.

'Flora, why are you so lonely?'

The question comes out of nowhere. All that bubbling, good-natured energy disappears. I twist further into my robes, feel their reassuring weight over my arms, my chest.

'I'm not lonely,' I reply quickly. Maybe too quickly. The implication makes me uneasy. 'What a strange thing to say.'

'But you are good company. I cannot help but wonder why you do not have more companionship.'

I suppose it is a compliment of sorts, though it's tied to a thought I don't much care for. I shrug, making it not matter.

'Why is it you read *The Count of Monte Cristo*?' Bram continues.

I frown. What's that got to do with anything?

'I read it because I enjoy it. Because it's rich and involved and exciting.'

'That's true. But could it also be that you relate to someone in exile?'

I open my mouth to protest, then close it again. That's not why I started reading it. At least, I don't think so.

The Count of Monte Cristo is about a man, Dantès, betrayed and locked away for years, losing everything. When he escapes, he rebuilds himself with a new name, a plan, and a hunger for vengeance. I've always felt like I understood him: not for the revenge, but for the feeling of being set apart, even when surrounded by other people. Of carrying a secret.

I bristle at the idea that Bram might have a point.

There's a pretty line of mosaic tiles to follow as we cross into a courtyard, and I become absorbed by them. A dry fountain sits at the centre as a point of convergence, surrounded by tables where old men are playing three-sided chess. They give us a passing glance as we stop to take in their game, but we're not as interesting as their wooden battalions.

'I'm not lonely,' I repeat, watching one of the players stretch out an overlong, age-withered hand to move what might be a rook across the length of the board. 'Besides, I don't need anyone.'

Bram leans in close. 'We all need others, Flora. We cannot exist alone.'

He says it in a whisper, a thought slipping straight into my mind. I shudder, not at what he says but how he says it, the weight of proximity, the warm sensation of his breath on my skin. There's something in his scent, something electric, like static humming at my fingertips. It's too much. I hold my breath until he's moved away, leaving me alone in the charged atmosphere.

Of course, I am able to doubt myself quickly, reason that I must have imagined the warmth, the closeness. I turn to look for Bram, and he is taking in the mosaic pattern of the fountain, light and dark blue tiles interspersed with white, an intricate sun design at the base. I wish it were running water. It might be soothing.

'Is that why you asked me to travel with you?' I ask. 'Because you're lonely too?'

Bram smiles that unfathomable smile of his, and I know he's not going to answer.

'It's getting late,' he says, gesturing towards the far wall where two doors stand: one wide and intricately carved, the other glinting like a mirage beside it. 'I think we need to get you home.'

A man in dark saffron robes holds a protective stance in front of the wider door, surely a bodyguard, and this is the entrance to some palace or monastery. He looks perplexed as we head for our own shimmering door, shifting on his feet to assert his presence.

I can only imagine the look of surprise on his face as we cross an unseen threshold, leave him behind.

It really is late when we return to the library, the darkness outside closing in around the building as though it's the last place on Earth. I try to protest that it's not all that late, but my stomach betrays me by letting out a ravenous gurgle.

'You should have eaten the grapefruit,' Bram says with a grin as he guides me to the front door. I'm not sure if he's concerned for me or trying to get rid of me. I still don't know if that moment in the courtyard was something or if I wanted it to be something. Did I want it to be something?

I flush at my confusion, exposed now without my protective robes. At the point of parting, I'm not sure what to say. Bram seems equally reticent.

'Will I see you tomorrow?' I ask.

'I will be here,' he replies in a tone that gives nothing away.

Barely an hour ago, I was wandering through the most astonishing market in the universe. Now, I'm standing in Tesco Express, staring blankly at a row of Pot Noodles. I'm tired and disoriented, not just from the travel, but from the quiet truth that is unravelling, reshaping everything.

The library floor, Bram's arms wrapped around me. The courtyard in Pam Angra, Bram standing so close, his words like the breath of him inside of me. I close my eyes, trying to fight off the sensation of him, his presence still clinging to me.

What I feel is longing, sharp and insistent. It scares me. The force of it, but also the risk that it might not be reciprocated. To misread something intimate, to move in close only to realise I imagined it all. There would be no way back from that.

The question returns – how can I fall for a man if I don't know who he is? I still know so little. Magda told me more than he ever has.

And what did he mean, this thing about exile and loneliness? Is this some kind of game? Is he toying with me? I've been toyed with before, and I can't say I cared much for that. I'm not a player of games. I'm an ordinary girl with an ordinary job, living in an ordinary town. Or at least, that's who I was. I suppose that's what's changed. Now there are new worlds and a man who happens to be the most fascinating man I've ever met. If he's even a man at all. It's all so absurd.

'Can I help you?'

I didn't notice the boy in the Tesco uniform approaching. I've been staring at noodle pots for so long, he probably thinks I'm on something.

Can I help you? The question builds in my head. What help is there? No one can help me. I'm walking blindly into stupidity, and I can't help myself. My face burns. I want to scream, *no, you can't! Don't you see? No one can! I'm falling for a man who doesn't exist!*

'No, thank you,' I say, grabbing the closest pot and heading for the checkout.

10

The library is quiet when I arrive: eerily so. There's no sign of Lilly or Cal, and none of the computers on the ground floor are occupied. I must be late, though I can't remember being late before. Why would I be late?

I can hear a hum, like the white noise of an overactive fridge. But there's something else, a resonance that crawls along my skin. The sound slowly takes shape: music, coming from the audio section – old blues, the type of melody Aunt Bette always loved. *They call it stormy Monday, but Tuesday's just as bad.*

It's playing at a low speed, as though the notes themselves have grown heavy.

'Cal?' I call.

No answer, just the music's weighted rhythm. *Lord and Wednesday's worse, and Thursday's oh so sad.*

I'm not sure whose music it is. It's not Cal's kind of tune; perhaps Lilly put it on.

'Lilly?'

Nothing.

Heading for the service desk, I find an old manuscript with faint letters scrawled across it. As I try to read them, they blur and fade, dissolving into raindrops that twist and linger in the air. I reach out to catch one and feel it wet in my hand, droplets pattering around me in an impossible rainstorm.

What a strange place for the rain to come in, as if the library itself is weeping.

I decide to look for Cal and Lilly on the first floor, but the stairs are so hard to climb: each step clings to my foot like it doesn't want to let go. I lift and pull, lift and pull, as though the steps are sticky. Or maybe I'm just tired. I don't think I stopped for coffee today.

When I reach the top, I find Lilly standing at the edge of the recess, gaze cast to the floor. She doesn't seem to have noticed my arrival.

'Lilly? Is everything okay?'

She shakes her head, slow and deliberate. When she finally meets my eyes, I recoil.

Everything about her is somehow wrong. Her makeup is harsh and overdone, the elegant cat flick now a cavernous void, her crimson lipstick carved into a jagged gash. The deep red of her hair is piled into victory rolls so exaggerated, they look ready to topple her over.

'You need to wake up, Flora,' she says.

So that's it. I'm dreaming. It should be a relief, but it isn't. Everything is just slightly off, so close to reality that outright absurdity might be easier to bear.

I try to tell Lilly that I want to wake up. No sound comes out. I can't shape a single word. Even as her gaze shifts abruptly to something over my shoulder, all colour draining from her face, I have no way to ask what she sees.

Dread coils in my stomach. I know with terrible certainty that turning around will be a mistake. I have no choice.

Lord have mercy, Lord have mercy on me.

Bram is there, motionless, like a monument carved from stone.

At first, I think only of Lilly: that she has seen him, that she knows. But it's worse than that. Bram's expression doesn't belong to him. His features are stretched, as if his skin no longer fits, his mouth pulled into an obscene grin.

'Bram?' I manage to gasp, though it takes everything I have to scrape the word out of my throat.

Bram shudders violently, limbs twisting as his body undulates, boneless, something between a man and a serpent. The last thing I see before I open my eyes is his jaw distending, his whole body coiling tightly as he lunges towards me, ready to strike.

So many trees, more than there were people in Pam Angra's busy marketplace. We walk among thin pines and corresponding strips of diffuse sunlight, needles whispering in the light breeze, sharing their secrets. The air smells of fresh resin, and I am in summer clothes of light gauze and linen.

It's a tranquil place and I enjoy the sense of easy stillness. Bram is also quiet, wandering a few steps behind me. Once the library closed today, he didn't even ask if I wanted to go somewhere; he simply pointed out a shimmering door in the literature section and, naturally, I walked through it. Perhaps I have become predictable.

As the trees begin to thin, I hear water lapping, a gentle tide. I turn to look for Bram, who emerges silhouetted from a shaft of golden light. I haven't mentioned my dream of him as some kind of monster, though it was weighing on me. Being here now, it begins to lift.

Bram's expression is thoughtful as he gently tucks a strand of loose hair behind my ear. I suppress a shiver as his elegant fingers brush my neck.

'I hope you enjoy poetry,' he says. 'We've reached the Rhyming Coast.'

It sounds lyrical, romantic. I'd feel churlish to admit that I don't enjoy poetry all that much.

'We did some at school,' I tell him. 'Sometimes I enjoyed the rhythm of it, like hearing the magical patterns of another language. Then other times it was like crawling through a tunnel only to find a wall at the end, cold and impenetrable.'

'It seems to be working already,' he replies as I follow him out of the tree line and across pinkish sand. I go to ask him what he means, realising that what I just said was rather poetic. There may even have been a simile or metaphor in there somewhere. So the atmosphere here makes what we say more poetic? I suppose I can live with that.

'Wait until we reach the water,' he continues, 'then we will see the horizon stir, as if the earth itself is shifting from one enchanting dream to another.'

This makes me chuckle, though Bram has always had a polished, old-fashioned way of speaking, so it's not entirely out of character. I go to tell him so, but what comes out takes me by surprise.

'Speak softly, sir, on wings of light, where butterflies take silent flight.'

I cover my mouth. That was unexpected. So it's not just that the words we say take on a more elegant turn of phrase: our thoughts are translated into some sort of verse. I wish he'd warned me! I look at him with a mute sort of panic as he sits at the edge of the lapping, rosy water, rolling his trouser legs up to his shins in the style of an Edwardian gentleman about to have a paddle. How can he be so casual?

'Come, sit with me and rest. Regard the sunset glorious, best.'

I shake my head, hand still covering my mouth. Dear God, don't let me blurt out something I'll regret forever! I linger, standing, but Bram persists.

'Come, my sweet. There's nought to fear, 'tis you and me. The world doth fade and we're set free.'

My mouth is clamped shut as I sit beside him. I don't dare say a word, despite my urge to speak, to describe every facet of being here. It's really pretty: there's a multitonal sunset warm on the horizon and high dunes around to our left, dusted with silver grass. I take off my shoes and watch a gelatinous fish leap in and out of the water.

The silence aches, like there's physical pressure inside me as I try to hold the words down. It's too much – the sunset is too beautiful not to give voice to.

'I wonder still the way to find your reason, why you keep me blind. Tell of how it came to be that you sought travel, you sought me.'

I clap a hand back over my mouth with a sharp intake of breath. The last thing I want to do is lay my fears and feelings bare. I want to understand what Bram is doing here with me, but not like this.

I look at him desperately, trying with my eyes to cover it all up, take back my own betrayal. He doesn't look back at me, only stares out across the open water, watches another fat fish leap from the surface and plop back under.

'There is far too much to say. Some scheme or bind to which my thoughts might pay, could force your fragile human mind astray.'

What does that mean? He thinks I'm too fragile to understand him? Too 'human'? This is a new type of surprise. I expected he might tell me a truth about himself that I may not like, yet this place has simply allowed him to turn it further back on me.

'But all this strikes me as unfair. I ask you for a tiny share. Something very small, that barely has a cost at all: to know from whence you roam, a summary of home.'

Bram sits further back in the sand, a hand capped over his eyes to shield them from the light of the persimmon sun.

It's infuriating that he is so relaxed against my growing anxiety.

'But always there is cost. I alone am privy to the sum of what is lost. You desire some small detail, but tell me, what would be the scale? Where would it end, my curious friend?'

I sigh, tired of the game this has become. The sunset is growing bolder, coming to life, yet we are like shadow archers, sending our shots out from dark corners. I don't want this.

'It would end with my knowing where things start and where they're going. But as I seek alone, I may just as well go home!'

Standing, I brush the pink sand from the soles of my feet. Putting on my discarded shoes feels like a protest.

'I grieve, I grieve. Dearest Flora, do not leave.'

Bram sits up, but there is still some lightness, amusement to his gaze that is all the more maddening. I wish I could tell him directly that I'm going home. I'm exhausted from trying to keep up with my thoughts.

'You play us fickle and unfair in shallow bonds of love you cannot master. The consequences be your grim despair for ever after.'

I have no idea what I've said, like the words came through me from somewhere else entirely. Whatever it means, it shocks Bram. He doesn't say anything more as we make our way to a decidedly literal door, waiting ajar at the edge of the dunes.

Back in the library, I know that what I said on the beach has soured things, but I'm too angry to care that my parting shot, whatever it meant, hurt him somehow.

'You did that on purpose!' I snap, leaning hard against the shelf of poetry books, Keats and Plath lending me some weight. 'Took me somewhere I could only speak the truth!'

'I wanted to –'

'You wanted to force my hand,' I cut in. 'It was cruel!'

'However, it was the truth.'

He stands firm, certain of his virtue to the last. There's still a pressure inside me, desperate to unleash itself. It's not poetry, more of a deep, cavernous growl. I bite it back, poker straight and breathing hard as I head for the stairs. I can't even look at him.

'Flora, please listen.'

I'm trying not to listen. There is nothing he can say that will make me feel better about any of this. Will it always be his arrogance that pushes me away?

'I wanted to find a way to tell you that I enjoy our time together, but it has its… limitations. Not my finest strategy, perhaps.'

This drives me closer to anger. I spin back on my heels, and he looks shocked as I take a hard step towards him.

'Friends do not need strategies!' I say, almost shouting, enunciating every word. 'All you had to do was talk to me. There's no need to play some kind of… of three-sided bloody chess game!'

'What you want,' he says quietly, balancing to calm. 'It would be too much for you to deal with.'

'You don't know what I want!'

'You want to know me. Who I am. Where I come from.'

'Okay, maybe you do know,' I mutter.

'Flora, I can show you such beauty, so many worlds to discover and experiences to have, but you cannot know me.'

I throw up my hands with a harsh, humourless laugh. He must know that those ideas are at odds with each other. What friend seeks to entertain another while giving nothing of themselves away? More than that, they forbid any kind of interest? That doesn't seem much of a relationship to me.

'Are you familiar with the Greek myth of Orpheus and Eurydice?' he asks.

'No,' I lie. If he's going to bring it up, then he can explain it to me.

'Orpheus, consumed by the loss of his wife, Eurydice, seeks her in the underworld. The god of the underworld, Hades, says that he will allow Eurydice to follow Orpheus back to the living world, provided Orpheus does not look back at her until they have left the underworld.'

'But consumed by curiosity, he looks back,' I snap to get it over with. 'Losing her forever.'

'You do know it,' he says with the hint of a smile.

I don't smile back. I don't even understand the relevance. If he wanted to use mythology, surely Psyche would have been a better parallel: the beautiful girl compelled by an irresistible need to see the face of her mysterious lover and punished for breaking the one rule he had – do not look at me.

'Everybody knows it,' I say, glowering. 'I fail to see the significance.'

'Think of me as Hades telling you not to look back.'

He says this so darkly that I flinch. I am not Psyche, but poor, sorry Orpheus, because I am not beautiful and Bram does not love me.

'Hades was a god. Are you telling me that you're some sort of god now?'

He shakes his head, frustrated.

'First you say I may be the Devil. Now a god. How very limited.'

I feel the heat of the pink blotch creeping its way across my chest, the growl in my belly forming itself into words.

'That's humans for you,' I sneer with as much sarcasm as I can manage. 'Limited!'

Bram goes to speak, but I haven't finished.

'Do you know what? I was beginning to wonder if you sought out a companion because everything has lost its novelty, that you wanted to see your worlds through new eyes. Now I think it's something more like vanity, that you want a pet. Don't ask questions, just adore me!'

'If that's what you think –'

Still not finished.

'Perhaps you are a god, all they want is adoration after all. Well, you can find someone else to adore you!'

I'm not sure if he disappears just before or just after I turn to walk away. Either way, I don't look back.

My hands are still shaking when I get home. I can barely push the key into the lock.

Anger isn't something I'm quick to feel, but somehow Bram has managed to bring it out of me twice now. It's that arrogance of his, the way he talks about humans as if we're some lesser species. *How very limited.* Who wouldn't snap at that? Then there's the jibe about me being lonely and the trip to the Rhyming Coast, which, as it turns out, was less adventure, more lie-detector test. Intolerable!

As for the mythology… I can't even begin to unpack that. I know it's going to hurt when I do.

'Breathe,' I tell myself.

There's a letter on the doormat from a credit card company that's not for me. Until now, I've been putting all of The Black Eyed Boy's mail in the bin, including what may have been a new bank card. I thought it served him right and hoped it would cause him trouble, in the same way as I've been letting Mr Friday, the spider plant he left behind, slowly dehydrate to death.

Right now, I feel indifferent to whatever The Black Eyed Boy may feel. So much so that I open the drawer of the console table to store the letter. The postcard of Edinburgh looks back at me.

'Oh shut up!' I tell the golden lights, the gleaming river, before slamming the drawer and going to bed.

11

There's no sign of Bram in the library when I get back to work the next day, and I'm glad. I am looking for him, peering as far as I can into the basement before I step off the last step and doing long sweeps over the upstairs balcony – if it's for the purpose of avoidance, then it's acceptable.

I used to look for The Black Eyed Boy everywhere, on my walk through the park to and from work or wandering around the supermarket. I couldn't help scanning the periphery for that loose armed swagger.

I keep busy. What with the knit and natter group and a list of reserved books to go hunting for, I'm well occupied. It rains hard all day, so we have to put the bucket out to catch water leaking through the gaps in the stained glass window, which we try to do with a certain amount of good humour.

I make sure I get the shelving done quickly enough that I leave on time. Lilly even comments on it, asking me if I'm in a hurry, as if I'm the one who starts giving people hard stares at ten to six.

In the evening, I paint my kitchen a pretty shade of green. It's named Light Emerald after a moth I didn't know existed until I looked it up. It only takes a couple of hours – I'd hoped it would keep me busy well into the night – and I've soon put all of the pots and cups back on the shelves and spent a pleasant ten minutes in admiration of my handiwork. I even consider buying some new mugs to coordinate, though I mostly use the same *Keep Calm and Drink Coffee* mug I've had for years, so who would use them?

There's a tough minute after this when I don't know if I'm going to be able to stand it. I'm a stranger in my body. I'm a box of moths fluttering and frisking, trying to escape. I flap my hands to try to move the sensation on, and it does subside. I doubt it will last.

I don't want to watch TV. I need my book to occupy me, but I left it at the library. I can't face going back. Not now. Not if there's a chance of seeing Bram and falling back into that feeling: that I could go anywhere, do anything. He took me to the edge of the universe, for goodness' sake! Showed me worlds I could only dream of.

It's over now. The adventures. The magic. To cap it all, I was wrong about his interest in me. Not just unrequited, something worse. I am beneath him.

When I arrive for work on Thursday, Lilly is behaving strangely. She would usually be having her lunch in the staff room with one eye on the service desk, our brief passing of the time another of our unspoken almost-rituals.

Today, she is in her office adjacent to the entrance hallway, staring out the door as if she's in another world herself.

'Afternoon, Lilly!' I call.

'Flora,' she mutters, coming out of her daze. 'Good morning.'

Close enough, I suppose.

Lilly turns her attention to some paperwork on her desk, and I go to hang my coat. There's a long queue of people waiting restlessly at the service desk, so I have to get straight into the thick of it. It's twenty minutes before the line clears. So unusual for Lilly to leave people waiting like that, and I have no idea where Cal has got to.

I only have to wait another half an hour to find out what's going on. The library is quiet again when Lilly calls me into her office. Her tone is clipped, and I feel a terrible sense of dread. Have they found out I've been spending time in the library when I shouldn't? Is that why she's behaving strangely – it's my fault?

'Take a seat,' she says in a formal tone. 'I'm afraid there's no easy way for me to say this.'

My stomach turns a botched cartwheel as my mind files furiously through potential rationales. Could I make a case for temporary insanity based on my recent breakup? Am I willing to say I'm lonely as a means of keeping my job, that I've been here simply for something to do?

'The library is closing.'

So it's not about me at all, but everything around me. The converted car park in the town centre was a closer reality than any of us realised. By next summer, we will all be wandering around in a glass and concrete 'Information Centre' with more computer banks than MI5 and a state-of-the-art training suite. We will all keep our jobs (except Anouska, whom Lilly had to fire this morning) and have been asked to ensure we sell it to the public as a positive opportunity we're all excited about.

'I'm sorry, Flora. I know how much you love this place. We all do.'

'What will happen to the building?'

'Oh, I'm sure some developer is already waiting in the wings, ready to turn it into flats.'

I fold my arms, not out of defiance but to stop my hands from trembling.

'It's going to be okay, Flora,' Lilly says.

'Sure.'

But it won't be, will it? It'll be something else I have to let go of. Do I really have to lose every time?

There's still no sign of Cal after I return to the service desk. Once another lull sets in, I go to look for him. It takes a while, but I finally find him in the yard outside the back door, sitting on a low scrap of old wall beside the wheelie bin.

He's smoking. I've never seen him smoke before.

'She's told you, then?' he says. He looks as though he might have been crying.

'Yes. Are you okay?'

He's obviously not. He shudders, trying to suppress a series of sobs.

'Did she tell you they're getting rid of the audio section?' he asks, his tone bitter.

I nod. It's hardly surprising given that most people can conjure any music they like at the touch of a button, but it would break his heart for me to say it. In truth, it would break my heart as well. I'm not sure it's big enough to keep breaking like this.

'I'm sorry.'

I'm not good at comforting people, so we sit quietly together, taking in the back of the building, the sandstone dinosaur that will soon be something new. My gaze falls on the small window at the back of the first floor and I think that I might see a face there, a shimmer of bright eyes watching me, then pulling back, not wanting to be seen.

'Cal, do you believe in ghosts?'

'Funny you should ask,' he says in a final, smoky exhalation before stubbing out his cigarette on the concrete ground. 'When I got in first thing, there was a record on the turntable. I could have sworn I'd put everything away last night, but there it was, *Days of Future Passed*. If that's a ghost's doing, they have good taste!'

This makes him chuckle, cheers him briefly. I look up at the window again but no one looks back.

It turns out I can still travel between worlds. This place looks a lot like Lyrium, although I can't hear any music. Perhaps it's the cliff near Aunt Bette's place, but it's so tidy and *beautiful* – the water is shimmering sapphires and the sun glitter is diamond fish dancing to the surface. I'm floating above, seeing everything at last.

But silly me, it isn't the sea at all – it's a wide river. How did I miss that? There's a cave visible in the cliffside bank. I come to land beyond its dark mouth. I don't like it here because I know it's the entrance to the underworld. I shouldn't have to wait for too long, though.

'Orpheus!' I call out when I see my friend coming out of the cave mouth. He looks drawn, unhappy. I think I know what's happened, but then behind him comes Eurydice, her red hair pulled into a long plait as I remember it, brilliant flower tattoos decorating her entire body.

'You did it!' I say, throwing my arms around Orpheus. Still he cannot bring himself to be happy.

'I don't know who the woman is,' he tells me. He sounds desperate.

'Don't be silly, she's your wife.'

'How can I tell? They wouldn't let me see. They wouldn't let me see if it was really she who followed.'

I look at Eurydice. She stands there silently, staring at us, the flowers of her tattoos blooming and fading in rhythm with the motion of the water.

I wake up on my bed, still in my clothes. I must have fallen asleep with my cardigan scrunched below my face because there's a line of buttons imprinted across my cheek, and I can't move my neck.

Before I nodded off, I was reading my book of Greek myths. It's an old illustrated version I've had since I was a child, so it doesn't spare the audience – the sense of loss and violence is graphic. When Eurydice goes back to the underworld after Orpheus' curiosity gets the better of him, she doesn't fade sadly away; she is dragged away, screaming, by a horde of lost souls, ragged nails tearing at her flesh. The scene is from Orpheus's perspective, and in the background, there is Hades, a great stone pillar of a being with a big curly beard and a knowing look in his eyes.

This is what happens when you don't trust the word of the gods, his look tells us.

12

I'm on the service desk for most of Friday since Anouska got fired. It's good and busy – lots of people are renewing their crime thrillers for the weekend, even a couple of DVD rentals. There's not much shelving to do, so Lilly doesn't relieve me until quite late.

Lilly feels bad about what's happening, physically worn down by the weight of responsibility for those who love this place. The victory rolls at the front of her hair are unusually half-hearted. I want to tell her it's not her fault, but the right words escape me. As ill-fitting as the library may have become, we would all rather be here than in a soulless box.

There are only a handful of craft manuals and a vegan cookbook to shelve in the basement, so I don't need the trolley. I'm pleased about this until I get downstairs to find a pile of textbooks left for me to put away. Typical!

I'm looking at the catalogue number of the first book when the light at the far end flickers. I barely register it, just make a mental note to remind Lilly to order a replacement tube, until a creeping sensation unnerves me. I look up. I can tell there's no one in any of the rows, human or otherwise, and I'm used to the discomfort of this floor. Something's wrong. I can't hear the clock above me ticking, yet the second hand is moving along.

I look at the lights and follow the line of them to the far wall. That's when I realise that the light itself isn't flickering, something is flickering around the light. It's small, the size of a mosquito, but it doesn't move like a mosquito, rather pulses with the light iridescence of a soap bubble.

'What the hell?'

I step closer, holding the book in my hand. It's a thick textbook called *Antimatter,* and I'm fully prepared to wield it as a weapon.

The thing, whatever it is, doesn't seem to have registered my presence and continues to circle the light in some weird orbit. I'm practically below it. It puts me in mind of the darkness that chased us at the edge of the universe, and the alleyway in Lyrium, the sense of a night with no stars: not a soft, cloudy night but the eternal darkness of an empty universe. Is this a tiny piece of that darkness?

'What the hell?' I mutter again.

Suddenly, whatever it is darts at me. It's fast, but I'm faster: with reflexes I didn't know I had, I hold up the textbook and catch the thing between open pages, slamming the book shut as I feel it hit.

It puts up a fight, and I have to hug the book in my arms to stop the whole thing wriggling free. My heart is racing. I acted on instinct, so I have no idea what to do next.

'Give it to me, quickly!'

From the stairs, Bram rushes towards me. I hold the shaking book out to him without any argument. He opens his coat and places the book inside, as simple a motion as someone putting away their wallet.

'You did well, Flora.'

'Thanks,' I say, catching my breath. 'Surprised myself, to be honest.'

'I think this may have helped.' He reaches out and brushes the bat pendant of my necklace, the protective gift from Magda. My pulse quickens, and I take a subtle step back from him. He looks pale in the fluorescent light, his clothes now those of a dusty Georgian dandy, long frockcoat and tall boots.

'What was that thing?'

'Nothing.'

I roll my eyes in obvious exasperation. So he still wants to play his evasive games?

'Fine, you don't need to tell me.'

'I mean it is Nothing. The absence of a thing. A void.'

'I've been studying what I call The Void for many years.'

Bram and I are sitting as bookends on the first-floor sofa. I made a big fuss to Lilly about how many textbooks were lying around in the basement, so it would take me longer than I thought to do the shelving. Our usual pattern resumed seamlessly.

'I first came across it beyond the outer reaches. In all of my travels, I never saw anything like it because it has nothing to balance it. Even antimatter sits in opposition to matter, unreality to reality. This has no balancing part; it is simply a void, consuming as it chooses.'

So this is what chased us when we took the form of vapours at the edge of the universe – the same thing that caught his attention in Lyrium. I remember the fear I felt in its pursuit, that it had latched onto us and wasn't going to let go.

'And you can absorb it?'

'Yes. Something in my form appears to neutralise it, allowing me to study it.'

I know better than to focus on how this happens. I've tried too many times to ask him about himself, which is what created the rift between us. I concentrate only on this enemy of which he now speaks. He calls it a void as though it's some vast abyss, yet the thing I caught in the basement was gnat small.

'Is it one big thing or lots of little things?'

'More like small parts of a nebulous whole: particle fragments. I thought I had gathered them all, but some time ago the bats noticed something odd at the edges of their realm. It struck me as similar, a particle that was consuming itself but continuing to grow. They call it The Chattering.'

I remember Magda using that term as we left her realm. *We must talk about The Chattering soon.*

'And it's dangerous?'

'Potentially, yes. In the furthest reaches, it seems to remain dormant. But when it comes into contact with living beings… that's when it is unpredictable. Then it becomes a problem.'

'But it was in the alley. In Lyrium.'

'Yes.'

'But…' I falter. I'm not sure what I'm trying to say. Something like *we have to stop it*, maybe. But who am I to decide that? Who am I to act like I know what should be done?

'All those people,' I say at last. The words come out small, but they land heavily.

'I will deal with it, Flora. Trust me.'

There's not a lot I can say to that. As funny as it sounds after everything that has happened between us this week, I do trust him. He is an enigma and continues to conceal himself from me, but when it comes to a threat to the worlds he cares for, I do not doubt that he will do something to help.

We fall into an awkward silence. I'm simultaneously concerned about this threat, while also trying to hold off that lightness I get around Bram, because I dread the dead weight that will replace it when he is gone. I have no idea what he's thinking: his thoughts appear to be engrossed in the floor.

'Well,' I say in the English style of hopeful departure, clapping my hands on my thighs to drive the point home. 'If I can help with anything, just arm me with a textbook and I'll do my best!'

'You're leaving?'

I'm not sure why he's surprised.

'Yes. I need to buy a paintbrush.'

It sounds very prosaic in the light of our conversation, and stupid because I don't actually need a new paintbrush, but it was the first thing that came to mind.

'You are still angry with me.'

The flipping, fluttering moths that have invaded my insides tell me that of course I am angry with him. So I know about The Void now – that doesn't bridge the distance between us. Does he really believe he can make me his Orpheus and still maintain our friendship, or whatever this might have been?

'I'll get over it.'

I try to sound blithe, carefree. Or is there part of me that hopes he feels hurt by my apparent indifference? Either way, I stand, go to fetch my book from the hatch. Bram stands too, with the awkward formality of an outdated gesture.

The Count of Monte Cristo is waiting along with the origami heart. I take both.

'Goodbye, Bram.'

Once again, I can't look at him as I turn for the stairs. There's a tightness in my features that I don't want him to see.

'My name is Abraham,' he says.

I pause, confused. I already know this.

'Okay, sorry. Goodbye, Abraham.'

He hesitates.

'That's to say, my name is Abraham and I was once human.'

It sounds funny the way he says it, as if he's at an uncanny version of AA. I stop walking. Take a step closer. Not close enough to touch, but enough to show I'm listening.

'But not anymore?'

'I cannot say with certainty.'

I know what he's doing. This isn't an apology, not really, but it's something: a shard of honesty offered in place of one.

'How long ago?'

'I think two, perhaps three hundred years. I lose count.'

'Wow,' I say. It comes out flat, more subdued than the word deserves. I want to say something clever or even compassionate, but my mind's snagging on what this means. I would suggest that he must be a ghost, except I know he can't be. He can hold a book as he reads it, fold paper into hearts and dance like he's as alive as anyone else. He can hold me. He feels real.

'I never died,' he says. 'The details are complicated, but… something happened. Something that changed me. It opened the doors to other worlds, allowed me to take different forms, approximate styles from various eras.'

'Can you tell me what happened?' I ask, my voice softening.

'It's hard to explain. My physical self was… altered. But I was human. I still am in many ways. I wanted you to know.'

'Thank you.' I step closer, considering how this changes things. 'But why hide it? What's so terrible about being human?'

'The man I was…' He falters, the words catching. I'm afraid that he might collapse under the weight of whatever truth he's carrying. His hand presses to his chest, as though he's holding everything in, raw and unbearable.

'I cannot stand to speak of it,' he whispers. His breath trembles.

'It's okay.'

I reach out, trying to offer comfort for whatever anguish the past holds. When our hands meet, it's a recognition of shared pain, an unspoken acknowledgement that our connection might ease it, something deeply human. We are something to each other, and I no longer fear that I was mistaken. There is something heady in the thickness of the atmosphere holding us together, the way his jewel eyes fall on me.

'I am so old, Flora,' he says heavily. 'So tired.'

'Not to me,' I say. I touch his face, meet his eyes. There is barely a sliver of moonlight between us.

'Flora.'

He says my name like he's breathing the letters out in smoke. When he wraps his arms around me, the fabric of his coat holds me in twilight. He smells of ether and old books, of sensuous dreams you could never share and the endless, battle-scarred wastelands of time. When he kisses me, it is with the urgent hopelessness of a dying sun, lost to the vast patterns of the universe.

Later, we are sitting on the floor, heads resting against the sofa. I have no idea what time it is. Bram has been telling me about the worlds within worlds that I might never visit because I would have to be able to exist on a subatomic level.

I'm sort of listening, but I'm also staring at his mouth, watching it move, thinking about how much I like the word 'devour'.

'I wish you could come home with me.'

He lifts my hand to kiss my palm, an intimate promise.

'Perhaps one day.'

I can't believe this extraordinary man is here with me, radiant in the moonlight. Will I always feel ordinary by comparison?

I must have asked this aloud, because he answers.

'Everyone is ordinary until they do something astonishing.'

'But I've never done anything.'

'Flora, you reached out a hand in the dark. You leapt off the edge of a cliff. That's how things start.'

What can I say to that? He's right, I suppose. I never thought of myself as someone who wanted more. I didn't dream big or chase after anything. I was content, or I thought I was – going to work, coming home. Sharing a life with someone who never saw me, not properly.

'I thought I'd travel,' I say. 'Me and my mum, we always said we would see the world. But it never happened.'

'You have time,' he says.

'I am happy here, though, in the library.'

It's true. For the first time in a long time, I'm alive. But we both know it's more than that. I almost say it, that I'm happy because he is here. The words linger in my throat. The truth feels too soon, too raw. I'm not quite ready to hear it in my own voice because it will remind me how fleeting all of this is: Bram, the library, everything.

I kiss him once more. Soon, I will have to get dressed and go home, then I will wonder again what barbs penetrated the heart of this man, brought him to me.

For now, there are only kisses.

13

Dawn is silver and grey with creeping streaks of mauve. I'm walking through the park at a time I never normally walk through the park. There are only runners and dog walkers for company.

I'm aware, as I make my way home, that I have spent the night with a man who is two or three hundred years old. I'm going to rationalise it by deciding that his relationship to time is different to that of most other men. So is his relationship to matter, for that matter, but that's a detail I'm prepared to live with.

I would happily float the entire journey home if not for a wiry terrier running out of nowhere, yapping as if he cannot believe the audacity, which sends a flock of pigeons blundering from the nearest tree.

Reality. I watch the birds bustle away in their panic. Following their path through the lines of the sky, I notice a small bat fluttering across the fading moon.

I fall straight into bed as soon as I get home, exhausted. I've never been up all night before, so the brittle peculiarity of turning the day upside-down is new to me.

It doesn't take me long to discover the romantic swirls of half-sleep, though they don't last. I'm jolted awake by a crashing sound from downstairs, a pot breaking in the yard, next door's cat practising her gymnastics over the wall again.

I'm in the kitchen, the green walls so vivid it's as though the tiny emerald moths are all fluttering at once. Peering through the frosted glass, I can make out a dark shape outside, warped by the rippled lines of the door. It's small at first, the size of my hand, but spreads to something more like human size.

I pick up a nearby bouquet of dahlias and open the door, brandishing the flowers as a baseball bat.

'Magda?'

The Bat Queen is standing in my small yard, out of place next to the herbs and whitewashed brick, in a long black trench coat and large round sunglasses.

'I hope you don't mind,' she says casually.

'Er, no, come in.'

Magda is so tall that I would assume she'd need to bend low to get through the back door, but the room twists instead to accommodate her. My sweet pastel moths darken into peppered moths as she stands among them.

I look from my visitor to the walls and back again, putting down the bouquet that has now become an old-fashioned collectable ornament of china flowers.

'Wait,' I say, taking it all in. 'This is a dream, isn't it?'

Her reply is characteristically blunt. 'A dream. Not a dream. What does it matter?'

'Then why are you here?'

'Some dreams are mere shadows; others cast light.'

I shrug, too tired for riddles. 'Do you want tea?'

'No, thank you.' She looks me up and down in the manner of an appraising parent. 'It seems you were unable to heed my advice.'

I give her a blank look.

'You have stardust in your hair,' she says by way of explanation.

My blank look remains, a dash of puzzlement as I glance at a loose strand falling over my shoulder.

'Not literally. It's a roughly translated euphemism that means –'

'I think I can gather what it means. Is that why you're here?'

'No. Your relationship with Abraham is your own. I am here because I require your assistance. You may have heard me make mention of The Chattering when we met.'

The Chattering. The bat name for The Void. Was it only yesterday that I caught that thing in a book? When I reflect, it's as though I can still feel it wriggling in my arms, trying to wrestle itself free.

'Bram calls it The Void,' I offer.

'Yes. It takes a different form in my realm. We are driven by sound over vision, so for us it is a composition of absolute silence as absolute sound rather than an amorphous entity.'

'Riiiight.' I drag the word out because I have no idea what she is talking about.

'Wait a moment, I will send you a vision.'

I wait, glancing at the china dahlias that are coming into full bloom. I can smell their bitter scent.

Nothing happens.

Then suddenly everything happens.

A scream, not a sound from beginning to end but a tortured note plucked from the middle, an agony of gasped breath. I see it in lines as I would imagine black radio waves on a blood red background created like a child's chaotic scrawl. It is pain. I am on my knees. The scream is mine.

'Do you see it?'

I can't reply to point out the obvious, because I am collapsed on the kitchen floor. I have my hands over my ears and my head on the cold quarry tiles.

'Make. It. Stop.'

The image dissipates. I gulp a massive intake of breath, which tries to explode in my chest.

'You understand now what the problem is?' Magda asks in her deadpan manner, displaying no concern for my obvious distress. I sit up gradually, wrapping my arms around my knees.

'You could have just said it was bad,' I stammer, though it doesn't come out as sarcastically as I would have liked.

'I wanted you to appreciate the significance of it. Since your visit, it has become more volatile. My guards are anxious, and these are not bats who are easily frightened.'

'But what's it got to do with me?'

'I need you to speak to Abraham. I do not believe he is taking it seriously enough. He tells me he is dealing with it, yet I have no idea of his progress. I believe it is becoming dangerous and I can't have it.'

Her words spin around me as I try to reconnect with whatever reality might be. The cold of the floor tiles feels good on my palms as I lever myself up. The jackhammer pounding in my head does not.

'Couldn't you speak to him yourself?'

'You were easier to locate.'

She points an overly long fingernail at the bat pendant of my necklace. It quivers at her motion.

'You're tracking me?'

'Bats can always locate other bats.'

There's so much I could say to that. All I manage is a cynical, 'Great!'

Magda looks as though she has more to say, but the back door swings open and we both look out into the yard.

Bats are waiting, at least a hundred of them, clicking and chirping to each other as they hover or squat among the potted herbs. Half a dozen are hanging from the bistro table with the casual ease of people waiting for a bus.

Seeing them watch me with their practised sort of indifference is discomforting. They are the visitors, yet I feel I ought to apologise for disturbing them.

'I have to go,' Magda says. 'It will be too light to travel soon. Until next time, Flora.'

Her coat flaps behind her as she turns to the door. When she crosses the threshold, she is no longer in her human form.

As dawn blossoms slowly into morning, I watch the Bat Queen dive into the pearlescent sky, followed by the papery flutter of her colony.

14

I wake with a jolt, and my bedroom seems unfamiliar. It takes me a while to adjust to the plain magnolia walls, the comforting calico bedding. The overgrown spider plant, Mr Friday, is silhouetted in the window and, with my sense of unease, looks like a stubby intruder with bad hair. I throw what remains of my glass of water into his pot.

Magda. My dream comes flooding back when I open the curtains. Too much light. My head pounds. But was it a dream? I can sense the scarlet and black scrawl as if it is written on my eyelids, the vividness of the Bat Queen's presence.

I need you to speak to Abraham. I do not believe he is taking it seriously enough.

He seemed serious enough in the library after we found that piece of The Void, but Magda has known Bram for a long time, and I trust her judgement. If she's asked me to help, even in a dream, that's what I should do.

It takes me all afternoon and the better part of the evening to feel well enough to return to the library. I make an effort to get out of bed two or three times before it sticks, but the pain in my head is too much each time. The painkillers I take get wedged in my parched throat. I can taste their bitter ghost all the time I shower.

Walking home this morning, I'd felt an odd lightness that detached me from the routine motions of daily life, as if I were observing it all from a distance. Now, as I head in the opposite direction, lurking concerns begin to intrude. What if Bram is cold again? Colder than when he was playing Hades, hard as stone? What if he's regretful? Could I have disappointed him?

Bram is in the basement when I arrive at the library, and my concerns are quickly overtaken by my reaction to the explosion of books he's sitting in. He must have taken every physics book he could find off the shelf: every textbook, idiot's guide, and pop-science paperback is spread out half-digested on the floor, along with several mathematics textbooks and a book called *Nature's Chemistry*.

'What's going on in here?'

'Flora!'

He's pleased to see me, which I'm glad about, but the mess he's made is inexcusable!

'Please forgive my disorder,' he says when he notices my scowl. He looks as he did when I first met him, Victorian coat and necktie.

'What are you doing?'

The look on his face suggests it's obvious.

'Reading.'

'Do you always make such a mess?'

'It depends. Sometimes I like to read stories. Other times I study, so I need many sources at once. It's astonishing what people take for granted that would have been heresy in my day. Look, paperbacks!'

He shows me Carl Sagan's *Cosmos* and Stephen Hawking's *A Brief History of Time*, in awe of their ordinariness.

'You're interested in physics?'

'It was my work, a long time ago.'

'You're a scientist?'

I sound surprised, though I have no reason to be. It's not some great twist, just a detail I hadn't imagined. He hasn't exactly been forthcoming until now.

'We were more like natural philosophers at the time, but I hope that my work would have sown the seed of what came later, had I been able to complete it.'

Things begin to click into place.

'So when you said something happened that changed your form, it was some kind of, what, experiment that went wrong?'

'I would be inclined to call it an experiment that went right,' he says, a touch defensively, before conceding, 'although lacking the corporeal means to prove it was, of course, unhelpful.'

Casting my eyes over the books scattered around us, I realise I'm glimpsing the side of Bram I didn't know about. Without evidence to the contrary, I suppose I had attributed his travels, his very essence, to a sort of *magic*. Now I see something in it that, though bewildering to me, is oddly tangible.

'You're a man out of time,' I say.

'I suppose I am.'

The concept is limited, but he likes it. He kisses me and I forget all about physics, formless states and even gravity, at least for a while. I've never felt so blissfully happy. But something is gnawing, a whisper at the back of my head reminding me I'm forgetting something important.

'The bats!' I say suddenly.

I tell Bram about my visit from Magda. Or rather, my dream visit from Magda. Most of it. Her presence is slipping away:

the sense of her standing in my kitchen (was she holding a bunch of flowers?), my pendant fluttering, a glimpsed image of hundreds of bats lining the yard.

I remember the vision of The Chattering well enough, though. How could I ever forget that pain ripping through me?

'What was it like, The Chattering?'

'I'd say it was like the sound of someone scribbling hard on a piece of paper and I was the piece of paper.'

Bram looks thoughtful.

'I will need to see Magda once more. It may be a good idea to visit Lyrium again first – see for certain what was in that alley. We can do that tomorrow.'

Tomorrow. I become aware of the hard tick of the clock on the wall, time moving on. What will he do when the library is gone, its guts ripped out, and the space converted into flats? Will he banish himself to his other worlds, never coming home? Or will he stay and drift from one apartment to the next, his gaze caught by the flickering TV screens, searching for solace in distractions that pale in comparison to the comfort he found among the books?

'Bram, did you know the library's not going to be here for much longer?'

'Of course.'

His matter-of-fact tone throws me.

'Doesn't it upset you? This is your home, of sorts.'

He shrugs it off far more readily than I would have expected. He doesn't look sad at all. If anything, he seems oddly cheerful.

'Come with me,' he says. 'I want to show you something.'

'Okay, but only when you've put *all* of these books away.'

We are at the far end of the audio section, facing the back wall. There's a cheap watercolour print of the riverside in front of me that I suppose is quite nice, but if this is what Bram wanted to show me, it's pretty underwhelming.

'Is there a door I can't see?'

'This one needs a key.'

He holds out a large iron key that looks as though it would open a heavily guarded treasury, and drops it into my right palm. It sizzles as it lands, quickly disappearing but leaving behind a key-shaped mark on my skin.

'Ow!' I cry. 'You could have warned me!'

'A small price,' he replies.

I'm left with something that is not quite a scar, just the faintest shadow of an imprint where the key was. At first, I don't notice any change – no door appears, no shimmering portal leads me anywhere new. I'm about to say as much when the wall before me begins to shift. It doesn't vanish; instead, it forms an outline, like the key pattern in my palm. Through this outline, a huge flight of stairs spirals upward, winding in a sweeping curve of thick red carpet.

'Oh… my…'

I peer through the centre of the staircase. There are two upper floors, each flight surrounded by tall white walls from which portraits of old men glare at me.

'You're seeing things as I see them,' Bram explains. 'This is the original building. I can take form both here and in your newer library. It's something of a palimpsest.'

I raise an eyebrow at such a fancy word.

'Palimpsest is the layering of new onto old. As time passes, newer buildings are imposed on earlier ones.'

'You were here when the original building was…' What's the right word? Here? Real?

'This is the Athenaeum. It was here before your library and is still part of its fabric. Whatever comes next will always hold an imprint of what came before. A palimpsest.'

I look upstairs once more, avoiding the eyes of the stuffy old gentlemen. I bet they don't like me being here.

Turning back, the ground floor is an ornate reading room, rich teal walls below a high, ostentatious plasterwork ceiling. Opulent medallions encircle huge chandeliers above a carpet of geometric swirls of blue and gold. In bays of neo-classical columns, there are shelves of hardback books interspersed with comfortable armchairs. It has the feel of an exclusive club.

I hold my arms out, spinning through the wide space like a top.

Bram laughs. 'You would have been banned for behaving that way in my day!'

'I would have been banned *full stop* in your day!'

Like a child playing, I balance along the swirling golden lines of the carpet, as if stepping on the dark background would send me tumbling into the abyss. I run my hand over the studded backs of the leather armchairs and take in the rich texture of the fluted columns with my fingertips. I want to touch everything in here. Open every book. Try out every chair.

'You spent a lot of time here?' I ask.

'Indeed. I had my own workroom upstairs. Meals were served through here.'

I follow him into a grand dining hall, another high ceiling with intricate plasterwork and walls of warm, buttery yellow. An enormous mahogany dining table capable of seating at least twenty people takes centre stage, adorned with a white linen tablecloth and a centrepiece of ornamental flowers in a wide silver vase.

I'm about to move a dining fork laid on the table a millimetre out of place, when a shadow flickers in front of me, as if someone is fanning their fingers in my face. The sensation is fleeting, but it's enough to startle me. Perhaps, in that moment, I was a vagabond ghost: a ghost of the future, haunting the great men of the past.

'Old shadows,' Bram says when he sees me flinch. 'I am alone here, for the most part, but sometimes a strong energy might break through for a moment.'

'That must be lonely,' I say.

'Yes.'

He's never admitted this before. To watch him pause, look up at the ceiling as if listening for echoes, not trying to guide or show me something, is new. Being in this place, as it was in his lifetime, marks another shift, which is more than I could have hoped for. More than just seeing the building, it means understanding him.

'A building serves no purpose without people,' he continues. 'Walls may remember voices. Floors may remember footsteps. But without someone to walk the halls, it soon fades.'

I'm sure he's right. But for me, now, it doesn't matter what's left to remember. The only person I want is him. The only voice I want to hear is his.

We walk back to the staircase and, as we ascend, Bram tells me more about the Athenaeum movement as the forerunner of libraries, a place for scientifically and artistically minded gentlemen of the day to pursue their enlightened interests. It sounds pompous to me because, if I had lived in those days, they wouldn't have let me near the place, unless it was to scrub the floors. I prefer libraries as they are now. Even if they are mostly taken up by computer desks with people streaming TV shows, at least everyone is welcome.

On the first floor, we follow a corridor to the front of

the building. This is where my recess with the sofa and the rose window would be, but there is no evidence of the castellated tower.

I miss my beautiful window and, as I think of it, the moonlit rose pattern spreads across the floor at my feet. The sofa and lamp appear faintly, fitting beside the Athenaeum's map cabinet. It's strange to see the interplay between the two spaces, like one trying to remember the other. It reminds me that I am in the past, except it is the present. You could drive yourself mad trying to apply logic to it all.

There are more books on this floor, in dark wooden rows, as well as private reading rooms and a lounge with the biggest fireplace I've ever seen. Thick carpets patterned with flame red ferns and the softest leather armchairs fill the space. I can picture men of adventure coming back from far-off lands to sit in here and one-up each other about their escapades. How I envy them.

There is a further floor to the Athenaeum that doesn't exist at all in the library.

'Close your eyes,' Bram says as we reach the upper landing. I do as he asks, letting him guide me wherever we are going, though I hold my hands out in front as if I'm playing blind man's buff.

I hear a door open, smell the scent of polished wood and vanilla. When I open my eyes, it is as though the night sky has been turned upside down. So many candles, all set out across a wooden floor that stretches further than I can see.

'The ballroom,' he says.

We dance. As we move, a tune begins to play, an old masquerade waltz I used to conjure in my dreams. Only this is not a dream, and there are no masks.

Turning our circles, we know as much as we need to about who we are, here in our palimpsest of shifting realities.

15

It's daytime in Lyrium, and the musical winds drive us to the harbour. I'm wearing a tea-green dress with a fitted jacket and voluminous ruffled skirt. It's a busy ensemble, but I like it. Bram has an Edwardian sense to his style today, with a high-necked waistcoat and top hat.

I never wanted my night in the Athenaeum to end. As pleasant as our current surroundings are, in my head I am still dancing across the ballroom, twirling like whispers of smoke from the thousand candles.

Now we are among crowds of people out in their finery. There's an anticipatory sense in the air, melodic chatter from everywhere. Children in sailor suits run around with paper kites shaped like boats. Ladies hold parasols and wear flowers in their hair or wound into extravagant hats. The weather is perfect. I grip hard to Bram's hand, sharing the excitement.

'Where are we going?' I ask. I'd forgotten about the singing sensations of Lyrium, speech as a scale of notes tinkling around me.

'The river. It must be the regatta.'

We continue to be swept along with the crowd until we get to the harbour. The shining water holds every vessel I could imagine: tall ships with pillowy white sails, handsome yachts and zippy rowboats that drag the river's reflection of the colourful riverside buildings across the water's surface, turning it into a piece of abstract art.

Everyone is excited. I'm excited too. But isn't there something we're meant to do?

'The alley,' I say. 'We're supposed to be looking for particles of The Void.'

'Oh, there's plenty of time for that,' Bram replies. 'You'll love the regatta. There are races and exhibitions and fairground rides and wonderful food. Oh, I think there's a race starting!'

We're not in the right place to watch the start of the race, but I hear an excited virtuoso violin of a compere over a loudspeaker, giving us the progress of four teams of rowers making their way down river. I crane my neck to see.

'And Pennymiles are out in front with Waterford in second!' the compere fires rapidly. I picture him as a squat man in a striped suit and straw boater. His hat probably falls off when he gets overexcited. 'But look, Roseleaf aren't going down without a fight!'

Bram folds his arms around my waist, resting his head on mine. I close my eyes. When I open them again, I catch sight of an old couple who have made a camp for themselves at the river's edge, deck chairs inches from the water.

'Battenmaus are trying hard, but still not making the headway they need to catch the others!'

The old couple aren't paying much attention to the race, despite having a prime position. They might have been watching races all morning, and it's become moving wallpaper to them. I watch the woman hand the man a plate of sandwiches, and he takes it from her while topping up her glass of wine. Their conversation is seamless, their movements so everyday that sharing food or topping up a wine glass means nothing at all. For some reason, I find this perplexing.

'And Roseleaf, Roseleaf have nudged into second! Can they catch Pennymiles?'

The boats come into view now. The first pointed bow passes us. There is little space between them.

'No, it's Pennymiles! Pennymiles for the win!'

The crowd around us howls and cheers with delight. It's such an exciting burst of energy that I join in. Bram gives a whoop of celebration that spins into a wild jazz riff. The joy rises like a tide, lifting everyone in a shared moment, until the last notes fade and a quiet warmth settles among us.

'Are you hungry?' Bram asks as the triumphant mood relaxes.

I'm watching the old couple by the bank again, how their conversation continues like there is no one else around.

'Flora?'

'Hmm?'

'Food?'

I blink, come back to him.

'Oh. Sure.'

The food stands are further along the riverside, set back from the racing path in the shadow of a big wheel and a striped helter-skelter. Pastel horses turn on carousels to the nostalgic melodies of mechanical organ music. There's cotton candy, doughnuts and funnel cakes topped thick with icing sugar.

Bram gets us cotton candy, and we keep walking along the river, away from the crowds as another race starts. It's wilder out here, the pavements of the city giving way to wooden boardwalks and sand lined with sea cabbage and hardy yellow flowers.

Bram eats his cotton candy by rolling it into balls in his long fingers, throwing each one into the air to catch in his mouth like a boiled sweet. I simply breathe in fibrous mouthfuls that taste of raspberry sherbet.

'You're quiet, Flora. Is everything alright?'

'I was just thinking.'

'What were you thinking?'

'That I'll never make you a sandwich.'

This throws him off, and he misses a candy ball. It drops through a gap in the boards. An ironically timed cheer goes up from the main drag as another race comes to an end, someone else's victory. We stop walking.

'What a funny thing to say.'

I suppose he's right, but it's also quite a sensible thing to say.

'I mean I'll never do anything normal with you. I'll never wash your shirts and watch you hang them out to dry, or cook spaghetti while you put out the recycling. We'll never walk home through the park or go to the cinema.'

He looks puzzled. 'Washing? Cinema? I don't understand. What are you saying?'

'I'm saying that you were right. There are limitations to a relationship with a man who doesn't exist.'

Why do I have to let this thought in now? On a beautiful day at the regatta, where the riverside smells of salted almonds and the commentary of life is pure music? Why did I have to see those people taking pleasure in the normal acts of everyday life, and envy them for it?

'My dearest Flora.' He takes my candy stick from me, holds me tight. I close my eyes, breathe him in. 'You want more from life than that.'

'Actually, I don't know what I want from life. I just know that if I ever wanted to build a home with you someday, I never could. Not that I'm any good at that kind of thing.'

It's true. I could blame The Black Eyed Boy for everything that went wrong, but when I think about it now, I'm aware of my own faults. Not that he behaved well, but I can't blame him for wanting more when I never let him in. It's like Bram said as we walked through the Athenaeum: we need others. Not just in the vicinity, but actively. With The Black Eyed Boy, our lives were separate from the beginning, bumping along together without any real connection. I should have realised much sooner.

'I had a home with someone before I met you. I was very unhappy, I just didn't know it.'

'Mistakes are part of being human.'

'Perhaps,' I concede. 'Or perhaps you were right and I am a ghost. Maybe we're both ghosts, trapped in a strange world of our own making. Only soon the library will be gone, which means that you will be…'

I can't say it, so I look out at the river once more. Another distant cheer goes up.

'Flora, I think you know, deep down, that someone like me is not supposed to be forever.'

Of course I know it. It's in everything we do, the fleeting nature of our fantasy. It's why the ordinariness of the old couple by the river seemed such a contrast to midnight waltzes in candlelit ballrooms. Romance is not made to last. But the thought of losing him is too much to bear.

'Promise me you won't disappear.'

'Flora –'

'I mean it. If you have to go, then go, but tell me you're leaving. Don't disappear as if you were never here at all.'

His expression tightens, and I'm afraid that he won't answer. When he nods, it is clear that such a vow is no small thing.

'You have my word.'

As the sun sets, we go to the fair. From the top of the big wheel, in a gentle evening sky of cobalt and ultramarine, the whole of Lyrium is laid out before us. The stars are faint in the low dusk, and I can see as far as the cliffs at the edge of the city. The streets are a tangle of bright, winding branches, like looking at an angiograph.

Our conversation at the riverside feels like a revelation, as though I've spent years pressing my hands over my ears to keep out the truth: that I also played a role in how things fell apart. Now the sound has broken through.

I don't realise I'm crying until Bram sweeps the tears from my cheeks. I let out a little laugh because I feel silly for crying on such a beautiful day.

We don't speak. We don't need to.

It's only when we circle back to the ground that I remember why we're here. I catch my reflection in the cabin glass, the gem of my bat pendant capturing the lights of the fair.

'What shall we do now?' Bram asks. I think he could perpetually occupy himself with all this frivolity. Magda might have had a point about him taking things too lightly.

'We need to do what we came here for,' I say.

'Oh, but the night is young!'

'And it will still be young when we're finished. We only need to have a quick look in the alley, make an assessment of what's there so that you can report it back to Magda. The fairground will still be here in a few minutes.'

The hillside piazza, where we sat and ate petit fours on my first visit, is busy when we finally get up the steep cobbled hill. We wouldn't be able to find a seat if we wanted to. I'm the one taking the lead as Bram patently stalls us, stopping to point out the view or admire something pretty in a shop window.

The café and bakery on the corner of the alley are both open, but there are fewer people on this side of the piazza. It's cooler here, the glow of the sunset unable to hold back the oncoming night.

'I'll go first,' Bram says as we enter the alley. 'Remember, don't touch anything. And if I tell you to run, you have to run.'

It smells more of standing water and metal dust than I remember. Bram is a few steps ahead, and I watch him for any signs of what to do, replicating the left-right of his pace. Then a shimmer turns my attention to the wall beside me. I didn't notice last time, but there appear to be gemstones set into the dark bricks, thousands of them glittering like fireflies, their light reflecting in my eyes. Or is the wall reflecting *me*, a thousand copies of my pendant all sparkling away?

I stop walking, mesmerised by my outline, reaching out to the sparkling image. As I touch it, I come back to my senses and see too late that the glittering gemstones are a mere trick of the light.

I've made a terrible mistake. There's something dark and gelatinous on my fingernail, small but deadly. I can only watch as it is absorbed into the skin around my nail, travelling below.

'Bram?'

I'm overcome with cold, utterly frozen. Everything crackles to ice around me.

I try to stretch out my arm to show him my hand, but it freezes midway, my breath trapped in an icy bubble that threatens to crush my chest.

It feels like an ending, filled with sadness. I wanted to go back to the fair. Now I never will.

'Flora!' I hear him cry out – a cry so desperate that a tear threatens to crystallise in my eye. The last thing I see is Bram running towards me, his own eyes filled with panic.

He reaches out, but I slip through his hands, falling backwards into the frozen nothing, a wormhole or cosmic helter-skelter that throws me beyond the reach of the night, digesting me.

I can't tell how long I'm falling. At some point, I am vomited up to land hard on a black and white floor.

PART THREE
THE VOID

16

I don't know where I am. It's some kind of hall, monochrome tiles leading to a sweeping marble staircase, huge planters full of fluffy white gardenias and camellias. A bust of Pallas Athene takes pride of place over an unlit hearth to my right, a Corinthian helmet perched on her head.

It is a light and vibrant room, like a stately home I visited on a school trip years ago. Everything gleams with austere precision. It is also vast: this hall alone must be twice the size of my entire house.

'Bram?' I whisper.

I hope he will find me soon. I feel strongly that I shouldn't be here. I'm no longer in my fancy Lyrium dress, and my ordinary clothes mark me out as an anomaly. Where am I? Is this some other realm or dimension?

'Bram?' I try once more.

Before me is an imposing wooden door with a heavy brass knob, perhaps a front door. To my left, a wide doorway reveals an impressive lounge, its gold wallpaper catching the sunlight streaming through huge windows. A smaller door sits in the far corner, beyond the bust of Pallas.

I try the front door first, pulling the heavy brass knob with both hands, but it's bolted fast. The weight of being trapped twists in my stomach, my mind racing with panic as I turn quickly, deciding which way to try next. Then I hear voices, people coming through the golden lounge towards me.

'Don't do anything that may disturb the master,' one voice says. A woman's voice, clipped and provincial. 'You know how he gets.'

I race across the tiles and duck behind one of the planters below the staircase, out of sight just in time. They look to be maids, two of them, decked in long black dresses covered with white aprons. One is carrying a large bowl of water and the other a pile of blankets. They chat in hushed stage whispers as they make their way upstairs.

'Well I think it's rum indeed is what I think,' the other maid says. She is younger and has a looser energy than her colleague. 'Those odd experiments he's always working on, it's unnatural!'

'No one asked you, Nora Higgins. You'll get us all in trouble with your smart mouth one of these days.'

'I speak as I find,' replies Nora Higgins brazenly.

'You'll speak as you find when it's well to do so, like the rest of us! Now, you just tend to the mistress and stop with your jabbering.'

She continues to berate Nora Higgins, their conversation fading away as they reach the upstairs landing and move along some unseen corridor. My relief at having stayed unnoticed fades along with their voices. I can't stay hidden behind a planter all day. I have to find Bram.

'What do I do?' I whisper aloud. I catch sight of the bust of Pallas, gazing left so that she is looking at the small door in the far corner. I remember from my book of Greek myths that Pallas Athene represents wisdom and insight. In the absence of any other information, I choose to take it as a sign.

I open the door as quietly as I can to peer inside, finding myself in a large study. The room is lined with bookshelves and anchored by a great mahogany desk beneath a vast Georgian sash window. It should be a beautiful space, but the light serenity of the hall has not carried through. Most of the books lie splayed across the floor or are stacked haphazardly among piles of paper weighing down a trestle table in the middle of the room. Beyond the window, green lawns are half-hidden by a thick blanket nailed over the view, casting everything into a dusty, perpetual gloom.

'Bram!' I cry with relief. He's sitting at the desk with his back to me, and I almost don't see him for the dim state of the place. 'Thank God you're here!'

He turns as I squeeze past the overloaded trestle table, which looks as though it may collapse at the slightest touch. He has been reading with some sort of old-style pince-nez over his nose, two lenses held together by a rivet. He looks at me so seriously that I freeze.

'What's wrong?' I ask.

He flinches at the sound of my voice. As I take a step closer, he recoils further to stand, holding the chair between us.

'What devilry is this?' he asks. His voice is grave, hollow with fear but also anger. Worst of all, he doesn't appear to recognise me.

'Bram. It's me, Flora.'

I try another step forward, but he scrambles for a wooden cane on the desk, holding it out as if it's a sword and scrutinising me first with and then without his spectacles. It's when he removes these that I see how tired he looks, dark patches sinking dull eyes and a sallow tone to his skin. He's wearing Georgian clothes again, dark breeches and a light shirt, though they're dishevelled, as if he's worn the same clothes all week.

'You are a phantom, set to unbalance me!' he rasps.

'I'm no phantom,' I say quickly. I'm trying to remain calm, but the whole situation frightens me. He frightens me.

I reach out to pick up a piece of paper from his desk to demonstrate my material reality. It is thick parchment with a spidery scrawl and some weird-looking geometric diagrams.

'Leave that alone!'

He brings the cane down with a rough thwack. Such is his force that he could well have broken my arm if I hadn't moved out of the way quickly.

'Ow!' I yelp, though he missed me – it's more from the shock. 'What the hell are you doing?'

'You speak of Hell, you vile demon! Go back then, back to the Hell from whence you came!'

He raises the cane over his head, and I know there's no reasoning with him: he's going to attack me. I turn to run for the door, but forget the trestle table, stumbling into it. My arms and legs flail as the whole thing crashes to the ground, and I scramble, unbalanced, over piles of books, bracing for the crack of the cane against my back, a scream coiled in my throat, ready to spring free and offset the pain.

The pain never comes. Wherever I was, I am there no longer, but have returned to the basement of the library, the clock ticking raggedly above me. The waiting scream becomes a single tear tracing its way down my cheek.

'You weren't supposed to see that.'

I thought I was alone, but Bram is here. He sits at the end of the aisle, slumped against the wall.

When I go to him, he tries to close himself off, wrapping his arms around his knees. He looks different to how I saw him moments ago: modern dress, but it's more than that. More than appearing less angry, he is defeated.

'I told you not to touch anything.'

The alley. It all happened so fast. I must have touched a particle of The Void, and it showed me a different dimension, a different version of Bram.

'You weren't supposed to see that,' he repeats in a grim tone, the dark pillar of Hades once more. *This is what happens when you don't trust the word of the gods.* So he really was Hades all along, and I was a foolish Orpheus who failed to look straight ahead.

'I don't understand.'

'Of course you don't.' His voice is bitter.

'Talk to me,' I beg, pulling him back to me, trying to regain the loving man he was before I looked away. 'Tell me what that was. You or something that looked like you tried to hurt me. Why?'

His form starts to shift. Is he fading away?

'No!' I cry, grabbing his hands to stop him from leaving. He tries to twist out, but I won't let him. 'You gave me your word!'

'Let go.'

'No!'

'LET GO!'

It's not his voice, or rather not just his voice. It's as if there are multiple Brams inside him, dark and light, hard and soft. He is every fearful thought I may have had about him, the dark god pushing me away for my own good, the charming devil beckoning me to risk my life. Yet he is also a man, a balance of those things.

'No,' I say again, calmly this time.

Bram tries to shake me off, but I hold on to his hands. He is surprised at my tenacity, his resistance growing stronger but met at each escalation. Even as his arm shifts to something slick and deadly, a snake's coils slipping through my fingers, I am relentless. A sharp, hissing mouth comes at me, full of venom, poised to strike, but I am a mongoose gripping with strong claws.

The walls around us evaporate, and we are riding into the air. His scales fall away to reveal golden feathers, an eagle's great wings folding through the sky out over the townscape. My fur and skin are thick, but I sense the swell of blood below his claws.

He tries to let me go, to drop and be rid of me, but I cling on to those razor talons until my own claws bleed. I begin to stretch, spreading up his legs and around his body, enmeshing his feathers as a wide net set to contain him.

As I hold on, I can feel what his fear is. All this time, he has been afraid of himself, the man he was. That's what I saw when I touched the particle: not a different version of Bram but Bram as he was, his past. It wasn't some tragedy that happened to him; it was a tragedy he created, some horror I do not yet understand.

The motion leaves his wings, and I wonder if I may have contained him. There's a fullness, my mesh straining at the edges as he expands, growing wider and wider into a sphere. He is vast, great mountains and seascapes pushing themselves through the gaps in my netting, trying to break free. He is a planet, an entire world making its way through the universe.

'I won't let go,' I say.

I loosen a fraction, enough to let my own bright form expand until I, too, am a sphere, a sun radiating for his planet. He cannot leave my orbit, exhausting himself as he tries.

Bram roars in frustration, the sound ripping through the air. We are back in the library basement. I'm no longer holding him, but I know he will not disappear.

'Flora, why will you not let me go?' he asks at last. He's so angry, but it's a tired, shattered anger.

'Because I love you.'

He looks stunned but shakes it off.

'Don't be naïve.'

'I'm not being naïve. I'm telling you the truth.'

'But you've seen the man that I am.'

It's true, I saw it all: the unyielding master consumed by his work, not in service to something greater but as a relentless obsession. He was a stranger to me then, a distant, loveless figure. Hardly the man who sits before me now.

'I saw the man that you were.'

I saw many things in that wretched place. I heard them too, like the chatter of the maids on the stairs. *You just tend to the mistress*. He must see it in my face.

'I had a wife.'

It hits like winter air in my lungs. I can't move. I can't speak. In all my enquiries about where he came from, I never considered what he had left behind.

'She died because of me,' he continues, spitting out each word as a punishment, though I can't tell if he's trying to punish me or himself at this point. 'I was so sure I had the answers to the universe, that I could find a way to bend nature to my will. But I needed money, a lifestyle that allowed me the freedom to pursue my work. So I married, but it was a loveless thing. I never even tried to love her. She died of pneumonia scarcely a year into the marriage, walking out in the rain, cold and alone.'

He is reliving it, his gaze fixed on some distant point, unable to escape the weight of his memories. I begin to imagine a lone figure walking through the rain, but she is not simply caught in a storm. She stands there with purpose, her presence a silent plea to capture his attention, a vain attempt to bridge the chasm between them.

'What was her name?'

'Edith,' he murmurs, the word shaped by regret. 'Edith Wellsingham.'

Now I understand why he wanders different worlds, why he has become a ghost drifting between realities. Over these hundreds of years, he has carried the weight of his failures like a shadow – unable to forgive himself, unable to escape the past that haunts him. In exile, like the Count of Monte Cristo. Like me.

In my mess of tangled feelings, sadness weighs heaviest. I'm sorry for him. And for Edith Wellsingham.

'I'm a doctor, a scientist. I could have brought her back to health, yet my neglect ensured her death. She lay dying, which I saw as an inconvenience. I left her, came to the Athenaeum to complete my work. I left her to die, Flora. Can you imagine that?'

I can imagine all of it. I picture Edith as some storybook heroine, Marianne Dashwood or Cathy Earnshaw, lost to the raging elements. I always thought them rather theatrical, but those feelings aren't so far-fetched to me now. I feel an affinity with the romantic heroines and the long-dead wife, knowing how easily my own emotions could drive me out into those bitter, numbing winds and how futile that action would be.

'I was a monster,' he sobs, slumping forward and weeping into the ground. 'I am a monster still.'

I rest my palm on his back, enough that he knows I have not deserted him. I remember him in my dream of a monster in the library, his distended jaw ready to strike. Then as the man in his study who lashed out. But it's not the same. It can't be.

'Would you act differently now, if you could?'

'Of course,' he says, pleading as if I could somehow make it so. 'Of course I would.'

'Then you're not a monster.'

He told me earlier that mistakes are human, but I don't think he's ever managed to grant himself such mercy. I'm reminded of a line from *The Count of Monte Cristo* about emotional wounds: *they may be hidden, but they never close; always painful, always ready to bleed when touched, they remain fresh and open in the heart.*

Whether he admits it or not, he is human, and this is the pain that proves it. Like the Count, Bram has seen the anguish that he's brought upon himself.

I say no more about it tonight. There are things he is facing, things that the centuries allowed him to evade. He pushed on doors into other worlds because he despised his own. He let his wife die. Ran away. Which is why that darkness, that void, let me see him as he was. See itself.

We huddle together, saying nothing for a long time. Bram rests his head on my shoulder, exhausted, and I put my arm around him, running my hand gently over his hair as he appears to sleep. He's so beautiful, even in agony. I watch him as the stillness slowly settles over us. I wish I could watch him for eternity.

17

My affinity with the classic romantic heroines has gone beyond reason today, so soon after coming into being. It has taken the form of two bus rides, a hike along a busy country lane and through what was once a lush field of wheat, now a muddy lake of charred stubs.

The rain seems more dramatic than it is because I left town in only a light jacket. I called in sick this morning, something I've never done before. Ironically, I expect the consequence to be actual sickness.

When I left the library last night, it was with the promise that I was not abandoning Bram. But things have shifted again, and we've found ourselves once more changed, this time sharing a truth that consoles more than it ignites. In our different ways, we now know ourselves to be in exile: me, from the confines of my ordinary life; Bram, from the shadow of his past.

When I got home, I couldn't help looking up the name Edith Wellsingham like some kind of time-displaced cyber-stalker. I have a bond with her that makes me feel in one part jealous and in another part devoted to her. I was hoping to stumble across a portrait of a rather plain girl with neo-classical ringlets in her hair and an empire-line dress, perhaps with a funny-looking lap dog.

There was nothing but a series of links related to Wellsingham Hall, a Georgian manor house an hour's drive out of town. It's not a renowned stately home and isn't open to the public, so I could only find a few grainy photographs of the building and scans of illegible historical records. There were no discernible links to the names Edith or Abraham, and yet I felt an irresistible draw to find out more.

Now, here I am at the entrance to Wellsingham Hall, stalking a woman who has been dead for at least two hundred years and may or may not have lived here, because I'm in love with her husband, a man out of time. How's that for obsession, Cathy?

The entrance is not quite what I expected. I pictured a worn stone wall, iron gates sagging on broken hinges, a battered sign lost beneath ivy. Perhaps a stone lion on the gatepost, eroded to fearlessness. Instead, it's a low brick wall and a fresh wooden gate. There is a sign, but it just says *No Trespassers*. I've come too far into this enchanted rainstorm to turn back now.

Wellsingham Hall. As I walk along the weed-strewn drive, I see the house, a symmetrical design with two long lines of six-over-six sash windows. Its once grand façade is weather-worn and faded, but it still has the bones of something beautiful. It could even be the more beautiful for it. Tall cedar and beech trees line the drive, and the lawn is wild but not entirely neglected. All in all, it's a tired place but not a forgotten one. The only flaw in the romance of the view is a glossy red Fiat 500 parked beside the front door.

I knock at the door. I've thought about this all the way here, whether I will be brave enough to approach. I'm wearing my work pass and lanyard, which I pull out of my jacket at the last moment to appear more official.

The door opens to reveal an old man in a tweed suit a size too big for him. He stoops to peer at me over his half-moon glasses.

'Hello?'

'Hello. I'm sorry to bother you. My name's Flora, I'm from the town library and I'm working on a research project.'

'Right?' He's direct but not dismissive.

'It's about someone who may have lived here. Edith Wellsingham.'

'Edith Wellsingham?' he muses. 'I don't know any Edith Wellsingham. You'd better come in, get out of the dreadful weather.'

'Thank you.'

I follow him into the hall. He's saying something about how it might have been a good idea to call ahead. Take a seat. Would I like a cup of tea? I hardly hear him. I'm too busy taking in the monochrome tiles of the floor, the sweeping staircase, and the bust of Pallas Athene watching over a small door in the corner of the room.

A new addition to the hall is a pair of 1970s velour armchairs pulled up to the fireplace. The fire is lit by a three-bar electric heater, which is lost in the grand aperture but welcome. I've hung my coat on a hook inside the fireplace, though my jumper is still damp, and my host has kindly given me a towel the texture of sandpaper to dry off with. I wrap it around my shoulders like a blanket while he goes to make a pot of tea.

I'm not sure if I can sense Edith Wellsingham's presence here or not, but it is the room I was standing in yesterday. It even smells the same, the scent of old money and disappointment. It is well past its glory days, with visible chips and cracks to the plasterwork.

I look at the door to the study and think of Bram, the terrible past version of him. I know there is darkness behind that door, darkness like the paralysing cold of the alley in Lyrium. I am afraid to look at it. More than that, it fills me with a deep, aching sadness, as if the weight of everything to be lost waits just beyond that threshold.

In my discomfort, I see Edith appear, ghost-like, in the chair beside me, the girl whose image I conjured last night becoming a reality today, all ringlets and pale chiffon. I suppose she looks a bit like me, the same age, but with more delicate features: sensitive eyes and a perfect little period drama nose. I don't want her here, and yet she has become inevitable.

'I certainly wasn't expecting any visitors today,' the old man says cheerfully, setting a tea tray down in the fireplace. He passes me tea in an enamelware cup, the type we used to get in school. I wrap my hands around it gratefully. How strange that he doesn't sit in Edith's chair but instead rests against the edge of the fireplace.

'Do you live here by yourself?' I ask.

'Good lord no!' he says with a jovial snort. 'No one lives here. I'm an archivist, part of the county team based here. My name is Arthur Tarweasel.'

'Tarweasel?' I can't avoid asking. I sense Edith giggling lightly behind a gloved hand.

'I'm afraid so.'

'Sorry, I didn't mean to be rude. I've just never heard the name Tarweasel before.'

'I've always found it a rather ridiculous name myself, though I'm told it's derived from the old English word Tīdwæs, meaning time-wise or punctual. I have no idea how the weasel snuck in there, though.'

I enjoy a light chuckle, my tea rocking so that some of it sloshes onto my trousers. Arthur Tarweasel reminds me of an old-style schoolmaster. Not an elbow-patches-and-flares type, but a proper *Tom Brown's School Days* kind of schoolmaster, with a long black gown and mortarboard cap. You don't get teachers like that any more. I don't even think you get people like that any more. He must be in his seventies if he's a day, but has an active, witty energy to him.

'Who owns the house?' I ask, more for Edith's benefit than mine.

'A local trust is holding it while we finish logging the archive. There is no family, so I would imagine it will go on the market once we are finished, become some godawful conference centre or hotel.'

He says hotel in the old-fashioned way: *ehtell.*

I nod as though I agree with the sentiment, though I always fancied a stay in a posh country house hotel. My holidays have consisted of staying with Aunt Bette or camping with The Black Eyed Boy.

'Now, you're looking for records of an Enid Wellsingham, was it?'

'Edith Wellsingham.'

'And what is your interest?'

'There's an old family link, I believe.'

Edith snorts at this and I glare at her. What is in her eyes? Reproach? Scepticism?

'Interesting. Do you have any dates?'

'Not exactly. Georgian period, I think?'

'Oh gosh, that is a long time ago. Any records from those days would be in storage at County Hall by now. There's nothing left here that goes back before the war.'

I sigh. Edith starts to fade.

'My interest is largely confined to the war,' he continues, 'but I can check the database for you if you would like.'

'That would be wonderful, thank you,' Edith and I say in unison.

Arthur Tarweasel offers to give me a lift back to the bus stop, which I'm grateful for. The thought of walking back through rainy fields in my current state of mind is far too dire a cliché.

As we drive away, I look back at the house. Edith Wellsingham is standing on the doorstep, watching us leave. We do not wave to each other, though we both know that we will not meet again.

I have a photograph of an official licence on my phone that Arthur Tarweasel let me take of his laptop screen. It is not good quality but enough to evidence the marriage of Miss Edith Wellsingham, daughter of the honourable Sir Jackson Wellsingham (deceased) and Lady Marion Wellsingham (deceased), to one Doctor Abraham Moreton. The year was 1820.

As expected, I can feel a sniffle coming on during the journey home. By the time I get on the second bus, my feet are colder than my hands, which are freezing. I welcome the sight of the town bus station with a sneeze.

As soon as I get home, I run a hot bath, trying to purge the lurking germs and get feeling back into my limbs. I pour enough bubble bath into the running water to make it foam almost to the ceiling.

I soak there until long after dark, turning over my understanding of Bram in the light of my growing jealousy of Edith. I hate jealousy more than any other emotion because it devours everything in its path; I can feel how much of me it has already consumed.

The first time I heard about 21 and Blonde, I was filled with jealousy because she was taking something that I thought was mine. I hated her for having the power to do that. Now I am her, only in a twisted way that defies reality.

The bubble bath scent fills the room, herbal and woody, and it reminds me of walking through lines of tall trees with Bram on our way to the Rhyming Coast: his fingers brushing my hair back over my ear, his presence overwhelming my senses. The memory lingers, not yet distant enough to be bittersweet – still pure, untouched by what I now know.

Eyes closed, I remember us as vapour, skirting the edges of the universe until The Void in its dark form came to find us. I remember it in the walls of the alley in Lyrium, how touching it took me to that terrible day in Bram's past, the day that changed everything.

A realisation makes me sit up with a sudden surge. My eyes snap open and water sloshes over the edge of the tub. Dread fills me with a restless energy that comes out in a startled cry.

I know what The Void is. But more than that, I know that there is only one way to stop it from damaging all of those amazing worlds.

And it breaks my heart.

18

I get to the library late, when I'm sure everyone has gone home. Bram is sitting upstairs on the sofa, reading *The Count of Monte Cristo*. I stand still and watch him, committing every detail to memory – the way the lamplight brushes his hair, the calm set of his mouth, long fingers curled loosely around the page.

'Do you think he ever stopped hiding?' he asks without looking up. He must also see the parallel to himself.

'The Count?' I reply. 'I don't think so. I suppose he finds some peace at the end, once he moves on, realises how much damage he's done.'

'So he changes twice, once to become the Count and again to move on?'

I don't answer. I don't want to talk about the Count; that's not why I'm here. Bram closes the book with care as I sit down beside him and places it on the floor, as if setting aside something heavier than paper and ink.

'I went looking for you today,' I tell him.

He nods. Of course he knows where I have been.

'You know the truth, then?'

'I think so, but I want to be wrong.'

'Darling Flora, how could you be wrong?'

I draw closer, take his hands. Time and reason may one

day force me to accept that he belongs to Edith. But here and now, he is mine.

'The Void,' I say. 'You have to gather every single particle before it's too late.'

He smiles. It's not a happy smile, but rather one of recognition: that he can be sure I know what the truth is. What is real.

'I have them. Even now, the doors between worlds are closing. There may be some fracturing while reality takes hold.'

'I will wait with you,' I say, giving him no opportunity to argue.

A door. A beach. The sound of lapping water. I haven't seen reality for days. My body is the sand and he the wild ocean. Touching. Savouring. I don't know this world, but it has the sense of a reprieve. I'm not sure where my thoughts are, blinking through the bleaching sun to find myself at the water's edge. Bathing suit. Pastel pink nails. Floppy hat.

'What will you do now, Flora?'

I have no answer. I realise as I hear the sound shake in his throat that the end, when it comes, will be prosaic. It can't not be. Life without Bram will be ordinary.

'Is ordinary so bad?' I ask. I'm not being rhetorical. I don't have an answer. Even the most commonplace thing can drive us to tears. The most conventional face can be beautiful.

'Hmm?' he probes. He looks like he belongs on a Riviera postcard, trousers rolled up to his calves, smoky sunglasses, but sounds like a teacher.

What will I do? Is it like what do I want to be when I grow up? I don't know. I think few people ever know, and those who do are often the most disappointed.

'I want it to be the day we met,' I say. It doesn't answer his question, but it's all I have.

'Why? Are you unhappy?'

I'm not unhappy, but he knows this will change when I no longer have my library. No longer have him. I know what The Void is, and I'm trying to be grown-up about it. Yet I also sense that my heart is turning to flint, that I'm going to start an argument for the sake of it so that it will push him far enough away to chase me, beg me to come back.

'I want to be able to meet you again. Then a second time. A third time. I want every moment to be the moment we met, an image in a prism split out and turned into every point in time.'

I can picture it, me holding out my hand to the night, and there is Bram, his gemstone eyes and hollow cheeks. *It is but a dream, a nightmare, that has disturbed you.*

'Why would you want that?' he asks. Not judging. Curious.

'I want that because I want love. To me, that is love.'

'Love is a stranger, hiding in shadows?'

'Love is a mystery. Love is the man who crosses worlds and wants to take me with him. Love is the man who fell through time to find me.'

'That is romance, Flora, and romance doesn't last forever. Don't forget you also want to walk home through the park, to build a home. There is love to be found there, too.'

'Can't you be both?'

We both know the answer. A kind smile is his only reply.

A packed amphitheatre. The dry sun parches our skin. Bram wears a wide-brimmed hat while my hair is turned up in braids. I fan my face and neck, clothes loose and thin as gauze. We watch the stage. The main actor plays Hades as a shirtless brute, voice bass deep.

'And the gods did honour Alcestis, who would die for love, and gave her husband back to her. But Orpheus, sorry minstrel that he was, too cowardly to offer up his life for love, was mocked with a mere shadow, his lonely death assured.'

'Is that true?' I ask. I've started to cry. Bram hands me his handkerchief. I can smell the salty sea air in its fabric.

'It depends if you believe that Orpheus was willing to die for love?'

'I used to think he would do anything for love,' I say. The theatre is crowded, but no one shushes us. The actors have frozen mid-scene, Hades' mouth a tortured question mark. 'But now, I don't know. He wanted his love, but he also wanted to live as he was, remain unchanged.'

The applause is unexpected.

There we are in the prism, split out in shades of pink and green.

'I don't know who you are.'

'No, Flora Cotton, you do not.'

He touches my hand, and the light streaks out into the night, an aurora. He is charged particles of earth. I am the solar winds. Together, we are a flickering display that covers the sky. These are not words but light understood as an approximation of words to continue the cycle.

'I don't know who you are.'

'No, Flora Cotton, you do not.'

Now I am running. The woods are fresh and dense, a tangled mass of conifers and spiky ferns, the air lush with the scent of damp bark and loamy soil. I love the feeling of motion. I have a fine layer of down across my skin and a tail that keeps me balanced as I spring across a great gnarled root, clipped lightly across the shin by a rogue bramble as I land. I barely notice, slowing to sniff the air.

I have him nearby, in among the range of scents, the sweet spot between fear and anticipation. I have him as I tear on through the nettles and long grass.

There's a building ahead, and I'm confused. There are no buildings here. But then, how would I know what a building is? That this is a house? His house. Georgian. I can hear music, chamber music that is old but hasn't been created yet. What is this? I don't understand.

I creep towards the house, stalking it. Sniffing the air. I look through the window and I see him. I see all of them. They are dancing. His wife is dancing. They have a house full of pretty dancers bowing and sweeping and twirling. I hate all of them. I hate him most of all.

'Flora?'

He is beside me. He is here, but he is also inside the house. The man inside is smiling as he pulls his wife into a reel through a line of clapping friends as the music builds into a bright crescendo. The man beside me looks tortured, sorry.

'Go away!' I scream, my poor little animal heart fluttering wildly.

'Flora, it's an illusion.'

'You are an illusion!' I cry. 'You are a phantom, set to unbalance me!'

'Flora, they are the illusion. The man in there could not be me.'

The man inside the house catches sight of us and stumbles. Surely this cannot be Bram as he was. The Bram who let his wife die. He would not smile. He would not dance.

Desperate to rid myself of the anguish inside, I let out a scream that could shake the night, draw down the moon. The tortured version of him puts his arms around me. I know him by scent, the sweet woodiness of old books, the sensual warmth of shared secrets. I don't resist.

'It's alright,' he says.

The house fades into the night, and we fold along with it.

We are back in the library, though I'm not sure that we ever left – whether I visited those fragmented worlds or they came to me.

The light from the rose window turns the floor a metallic blue, and a slight tremor makes the furniture creak, the lamp blink on and off. The cabinets of the Athenaeum appear and disappear like the silvery afterimage of a lightning flash.

'It is almost time,' Bram says.

Whatever happens, I will not leave him. But how do you hold on when everything you love begins to unravel? There are no tears, only the numb, pulsing tension that fills a body when shock outpaces sorrow. It sits like a scream held too long.

I feel him shift beside me.

'Let me show you one last thing,' he says, pulling himself to stand. He has weakened in the time we were held in those vanishing fragments. He looks sickly, dark circles trying to dull his eyes.

I move to support him, but he doesn't want my help. He walks slowly, and I follow, the room flickering between the library and the Athenaeum, the present and the past. The floor is unsteady, teetering on the edge of permanence.

We cross the Athenaeum lounge with its flame-red ferns and soft armchairs, into a corridor lined with smaller rooms. Another tremor sees the floor tip sideways, and I manage to hold in an astonished scream. We are tumbled through an open doorway into a plain room furnished with a small wooden desk. A tiny window on the back wall is the only light source. The simplicity is incongruous.

'I used to work here most of the time,' Bram says. He leans against the wall, and I have to stop myself from trying to hold him up, treat him like an invalid. 'If you wait a moment, you will be able to see.'

I'm not sure what I'm waiting for. As it turns out, it doesn't take long.

A ghostly version of Bram begins to appear at the desk, spectral before us. I'm afraid at the sight of him. He has that cold, desperate look in his eyes I have seen before.

The ghost works furiously at the desk. I see things fade and reform around him: a clock, compasses, reams of parchment. We must be seeing him over a period of time, so fast that at one point he seems to fracture like the light of a prism, and there are multiple versions of him. He is at the desk but also at the small window, racing in and out of the door at the same time. Pacing. Muttering. Thinking. Writing.

Then he looks straight at me, and I shudder. I wonder if he might say something, but instead, he throws back his head and the room is engulfed in a blinding white light.

I shield my eyes. When I dare to look again, a soft, lingering shimmer remains, emanating from the spectral Bram. He is transformed into radiant, unearthly energy. I realise what I'm witnessing.

'Your experiment!'

'At first I was elated,' Bram tells me as we watch the ghost of him pace the room. 'But I soon realised that no one could see or hear me. I was so angry. I wanted recognition in this world. I had transformed matter, bested all of those old men who came before, yet I was unable to speak of it.'

The light begins to dissipate. I am no longer looking at one spectral man but a projection of light sweeping across the walls, a kaleidoscope of colours and images playing out.

'In my new form, I could create doors that took me beyond this world, this very universe. I had thought my peers so limited, so rooted in the ordinary, but it was only when I began to share, to acquaint myself with other beings, that I came to realise how truly limited I myself had been. The best thinkers learn from others, always.'

I watch his past unravel like a film before me. There is Magda, a small bat and then a beautiful woman in her realm, Bram helping her to make it the place it became.

'The Bat Realm was the first realm I discovered. But I could not stay. All the time, my mortality was seeking me out, that darker part of me, the thing that remains rooted to this world. The Void. My life. My death.'

There's a dark patch bleeding inward from the edge of the image, unfurling like a living entity that wants to swallow up all of that radiant energy.

The Void.

Bram wasn't lying when he told me what it was, but he didn't admit the whole truth – that The Void is part of him, the darker part that anchors him to his mortal self. When he fully absorbs that mortality, it will be in its most final sense.

That is why my heart breaks. The Void will take him over completely, and he will die. There is no alternative. Mortally, he is over two hundred years old. He would never survive those years returning, but he cannot allow it space in the other worlds.

'Over time, I hope I became a better man.'

For now, his words keep the projected colour strong enough to fight against the creeping shadow. I see the richness of Lyrium, hear its music, follow the flow of the river further and further out. Vast worlds expand cinematically, and we hurtle through them with exhilarating speed. So many worlds, like the many stars I saw at the edge of the universe, all turning, wandering, colliding.

'There were many loves over the years: distant elements, dreaming princesses. I could never stay long, but I learnt what it was to love them.'

Gas entities flow at the far end of reality. Sentient words. Clockwork flowers. All of these things in unknowable places that Bram has touched. I watch it all play out around me, overwhelmed by a profound sense of connection to every being, every blossom, every tiny atom. The dark patch is fighting its way through, clouding the frame, but it can't take away that connection.

'The human world was a place I always came back to. I watched people come and go in the library over the years.'

The library shelves shift dreamily, as if glimpsed through the compound eye of a drifting butterfly. Snippets of conversation float past – curiosity, the search for understanding, for answers, for those invisible threads of connection.

'Then, finally, there was you. My little ghost.'

I take Bram's hand. Smile at him. The images are faded almost to nothing now, but before the darkness takes over, I see myself projected. I am on the moonlit floor of the library, shifting and turning to an imagined waltz, my laughter ringing out as I lose my balance and stumble. I see myself through Bram's eyes as I straighten, one hand held out before me, the other on my heart, eyes closed.

I can feel his hesitation: that in all his time drifting between worlds, he has not connected with another human soul; that my natural curiosity could reveal the worst parts of him, forcing him to confront them after all these years. And yet, he cannot resist the quiet pull between us.

His hand moves to mine as if sensing that, in my reluctance to embrace the future, his presence might offer me a glimpse of something more hopeful, more wonderful, than I had allowed myself to imagine.

As our hands touch, the image flickers like an old film reel sputtering to its end. We're left in the hollow darkness of an abandoned cinema. Bram coughs and stumbles forward.

'Let's find somewhere to sit down,' I say.

Bram is drained but keeps moving, dragging himself past the soft chairs of the Athenaeum to the sofa in the library, the place he most wants to be. A calm has descended here, and I could easily believe that the danger has passed. But as we reach the sofa, Bram is so frail, it is painful to see him.

19

When The Black Eyed Boy left, I felt foolish and cheated, but it was never like this. What I'm experiencing now goes beyond the metaphorical dagger in the heart. I am a piece of paper in a press, branded with despair; the patch of flesh hit by the tattoo needle, indelibly stained.

'It's not fair!' I cry suddenly, viciously. I realise I sound like a petulant child, but my beautiful Bram is dying and the world, the universe, will not let me stop it.

'No, it is not fair,' he says more calmly, the consoling parent. 'But it is right. I have been here a long time, far longer than I should have been.'

Tears well in my eyes, and Bram reaches out as if to gather them before they escape. I kiss his hands, his pale wrists. I wish I could kiss him back to life.

'I'm sorry you have to see me like this, Flora. It will not be long now.'

He is resigned, but I want to act.

'There must be something we can do.'

Bram chuckles, and it makes him cough again. 'Run out into your world and I'll become a real man? This is not that kind of story, Flora.'

I have no sense of how long we sit there, saying nothing, bathed in the light of the rose window. The moon is full and high, its soft radiance filtering through the intricate patterns of the glass, creating a subtle play of light and shadow around us.

'Why don't we go outside and see?' I ask eventually. 'At the very least, you will get to see your own world as it is now.'

For all we know, he might vanish into thin air or shatter into a thousand streaks of dark light the moment he leaves the library. Or it could be the version I want to imagine, where his pale skin is hit by starlight and miraculously transforms to beautiful flesh so that he can stay here, with me, forever.

I know he harbours doubts and sees exactly where my imagination is leading, yet he humours me with a tender resignation.

'I shall miss this place,' he says, taking one last look around as he gets up. He descends the stairs slowly and skirts the shaded edges of the ground floor's theatrical spotlight, no longer playing the exuberant trickster.

Time toys with me, making me remember the last time we stood at the front door, when we raced back for the thrill of adventure, as something that happened decades ago. Those imagined years have caught up with Bram, and he staggers. When I take his hand, it's to remind him that I'm here.

'I won't leave you,' I say.

'When the time comes, you will not have a choice.'

'Don't be tricksy.'

He is with me as we cross the threshold, down the steps and across the road. When we get into the park, he stands still and closes his eyes, breathes in the trees and expanses of grass, the air of the present, the sweetness of now. He is here, entirely, and I feel the quiet ache of what it must mean to him to belong to this moment.

We keep walking, and I shoulder the burden of him. We move away from the sound of the road to a narrow stream where the trees are densest, through to the wide lawn beyond the walkway. It is so quiet.

'Do you feel different?' I ask as we reach the middle of the grass, the heart of the park. I know he wishes he could tell me that he does.

The breeze lifts his coat, and his pale skin shimmers. We hold each other as if we are one, dancing to a melody that doesn't play, a silent song that lets us rise and turn gently among the stars. If I never see him again, this will be all of our time together, here in the park that overlooks the place we met.

When he crumbles to the ground, panic rises in my chest. I hear a rustle of wings. Three figures fold out of the darkness before us. Magda, flanked by two tall, humanoid bats.

My first thought is that she has come to be with him at the end, but then I see something hard in her gaze: a solemn blend of sorrow and resolve, the kind that comes from knowing what must be done. I see it, too, in the quiet menace of her companions.

'I am sorry, Abraham, but this has to end. I cannot let you damage my realm any further.'

I take in a sharp breath, cover my mouth. It never occurred to me that his end might come at the hands of those who loved him.

'Dearest Magda, the Bat Realm was the first realm that I discovered. I helped you to shape it as you needed it, shared precious time there with you, with Ralina. I would never let that place be harmed.'

'Then we know what comes next.'

'Yes.'

No!' I shout in protest, trembling. I can't stand this. I hover over Bram, protective, though Magda's hardy companions tower over me. They will not touch him.

'Flora,' Magda says as patiently as she is able, 'as long as you hold on, he will be forced to stay, getting sicker and sicker.'

'But you can't just kill him.'

'You heard The Chattering. I showed you what we are up against. If he lives, all of reality is in danger.'

My body is so heavy with the weight of frustration and sadness that I want to collapse into the dirty ground, but I kneel upright.

'He knew you would come!'

'He knew I would protect my realm at all costs.'

'Please, Flora,' Bram says weakly as Magda's companions loom closer still, leather wings coming for me, a blanket of darkness. I push them away, but as I am, with Bram weakened, we are no match for them.

Your realm was the first world I found. The words sink in, merging with what I remember from his kaleidoscope of worlds. *The Bat Realm was the first realm I discovered.*

'Wait!'

'Flora,' Magda sighs once more. She is tired, worn by heartbreak.

'You said the Bat Realm was the first world you found, the first door you opened?'

Bram manages a shallow nod.

'The first door? You're sure?'

'What of it?' Magda snaps.

'The Chattering. I think I know what it is. We need to go there, now.'

A flutter of wings, and we are here again, in the realm of ruby skies and jagged trees. I stand alongside Bram and Magda on the edge of a rocky slope. I cannot see the castle; this must be the furthest edge of the Bat Realm.

I am wearing a long, dark coat, heavy as my sorrow, which catches and ebbs in the powerful winds.

The Chattering is a vast and terrible thing. I can feel it in my heart as much as I can hear it, scarlet and black scratching across every frayed nerve. It appears as a hole in a cliff edge before us, a door to the underworld.

'You collected every particle of The Void?' I ask Bram, calling out over a sheaf of wind that whips up my hair. He has regained a little of his strength and is looking at the hellmouth of The Chattering, his gaze as dark and unknowable as the thing itself.

'All of them,' he replies. 'Only The Chattering remains.'

'Good, because I think we were wrong. The Chattering isn't part of The Void. It's a door. The first door. I think it will take you back to the day of your experiment.'

He looks at me as if I'm being naïve again, something close to pity.

'Flora, there is no going back.'

'How do you know? Did you ever try? In all the time you spent exploring, did you ever try to go back to your own time?'

He shakes his head. Like the Count of Monte Cristo, he buried that part of himself so deep that looking back felt meaningless. Maybe that's why, in the end, he needed to find me.

'Please, Bram,' I say, heart skittering. 'Remember when I touched The Void? It threw me back to a day in your past. Maybe… maybe closing this last door means going back to that moment.'

He looks at me, conflicted.

'I can't be that man again. Don't ask me to.'

'But what if you could be both? The man you were and the man you've become? What if you could change what happened to Edith?' I swallow hard. 'That house I saw. The dancing. What if it wasn't an illusion? What if I was meant to see that possible future – the Bram who went home, gave Edith the life she deserved?'

It kills me to remember it, the Bram who danced with his wife and looked out at us as our fantasy crumbled. Would that not be better than him being lost to the world entirely?

'But why would that future show itself to you?'

It's a fair question. Why did that image wrap itself around me? Why am I the one to love this man out of time: the man who found a lost girl in the library and helped her to understand her own curious heart?

'Because I'm the one who believes in you.'

I can see a glimmer of hope, as if there could be some twisted logic to it.

Bram looks at Magda and the way she looks back at him tells him to try. He leans in and whispers something to her. I think they even take their bat forms for an instant, flutter a spiral into the sky.

Then he is beside me. He knows I'm right. I can feel it. I have won and I have lost, all at once.

'I don't want to forget you,' he whispers.

I think of my bat pendant, how it might protect him. 'Take this. With any luck, it will lock the worlds within you, keep your memories of who you became.'

Bram takes the shimmering bat in his hand, and my whole world breaks. I am a mess of moving parts – too many, too much, the moths swarming. I can't keep it all together.

'Thank you, Flora.'

I don't say anything. I can't. I'm so torn between doing what is right and wanting to be wrong.

As he wraps his arms around me, the moths do their best to flutter back. I hold on. I've loved him more in these last few days than I ever loved the man who came before. I had no idea it could burn bright. That I could visit new worlds. That I could dance.

Holding on to Bram for the last time is like holding on to sand, but I try for as long as I can. He looks at me one last time, kisses me.

'Goodbye,' I say.

He steps into The Chattering without giving himself the doubt of looking back, and I am demolished. I feel a desperate urge to run after him, to go with him to the past. It doesn't matter that I might have a terrible life skirting the edges. Being on the periphery of him, peering through the windows of his life, feels in that moment to be enough.

Magda, reading my thoughts, reaches out to touch my shoulder, hold me in the present. We stand together and watch the scarlet chaos shudder, begin to collapse.

After what seems like an age, The Chattering turns in on itself and blinks into a spec of light that fades and drops to the ground in front of us. When I look, the piece that remains is the origami heart holding fast to its tiny silver star. I pick it up, hold on to it as if my life depends on it. The wind settles.

'You did well, Flora,' Magda says. 'It was good thinking. You would have made an excellent bat.'

I want to be strong, but her words break me down. I'm not crying any more, I just need to hold on to someone who understands, so I put my arms around her. This catches her off guard, but eventually she holds on to me. She may be crying herself.

We stand there for a long time, until at some point I take a full breath and straighten. This will end for me soon, and it would be impolite not to say goodbye.

'I wonder if he made it,' she says thoughtfully.

'I hope so. I'm sure we'll know, somehow.'

'You are welcome to stay here if you would like,' Magda says as we turn and walk away from this craggy edge. 'All of my children's children will welcome you.'

'That's very kind, but I don't belong here.'

She nods. 'Immortal realms are not for everyone. Even Ralina craved mortality, in the end. I wish you could have met her; she was the best of all of us. I miss her dreadfully.'

I think of my mum as she says this and can imagine her saying the same thing about me. *I miss her dreadfully*. It's not really the way she speaks, but that doesn't change the sentiment.

I give Magda one last hug. It is time to go.

'Do you know how to get back to your world?' she asks.

'Yes,' I reply, blinking, dissolving. 'I have a key.'

I open my eyes and am in the moonlit library once more.

I know it was real.

I know it was real because the memory of The Chattering is gnawing at my optic nerve.

I know it was real because I am gripping onto the origami heart in the place where my pendant used to be.

I know it was real because Bram is gone.

PART FOUR

HIS FINAL PREDICTION

20

I get to the café early, first thing in the morning. The only other people here are a couple of workmen eating bacon rolls in the corner and a runner who's clearly tired of exercising in the park and ducked in for a latte. I've had a little sleep but could have done with more. Surprisingly, I feel okay.

The guy with the tattoos is serving. His beard is tied into a plait today, and when he looks up, he's halfway through stacking sugar cubes into a small tower beside the till.

'Hi there,' he says, like I'm someone he's been expecting, even though we've barely spoken.

I decide to be adventurous.

'Hi. Can you tell me what the special is today, please?'

'Sure, it's the Rosewood Infused Latte with a Raspberry and White Chocolate Swirl.'

I inhale a sharp breath, then let it all flow out.

'I know it's really boring, but can I just have a cup of filter coffee?'

He chuckles and reaches for the coffee pot, pouring me the biggest mug I've ever seen. 'That's not boring. Why mess with a classic?'

As I pay, I notice that he's only charged me for a small cup, which is nice of him.

'You're early today.'

His observation takes me by surprise, and it must show. I go to fiddle with my bat pendant, which of course is not there.

'You work in the library, right?'

'Yes.'

My brain fogs up, not sure what else to say. I can't just leave it at that.

'I'm not usually in town this early, so I needed coffee.'

'Well, it's nice to see you,' he says with a warm smile.

It's not much, but I guess that's how things start.

I don't take the window seat, because I'm not quite ready to look at the library. I'm not ready to imagine it without Bram. This afternoon I will have to go in as usual, but I don't have to confront everything at once. One thing at a time. I have a lot to do before then.

My first task is something to get out of the way. I take my phone from my bag and find an old thread of conversations with The Black Eyed Boy. I have one final message for him.

> *Hi, it's me. I just wanted to tell you that you were right. It wasn't working. I don't like what you did but I understand why you did it. I don't hate you, I want you to be happy. Flora.*

He might have a good laugh at that. He might think I'm attempting some kind of double bluff, read a tone I haven't intended. He might even be sorry. But I can't control any of that. Whatever he wants to do with it is up to him.

I take a sip of coffee and relax into my seat. That wasn't so hard.

This next part is where it gets much harder.

Wellsingham Hall looks just as it did on my last visit, although it is sunny this morning. The sign on the low brick wall still says *No Trespassers*. A weed-strewn drive still leads me to the weather-worn beauty of the house, though this time a dark purple camper van is parked outside.

I am expecting Arthur Tarweasel to open the door, but am met instead by staggering familiarity.

'Bram?'

Obviously he is not Bram, but I of all people cannot miss the likeness: the same aquiline nose and unfailing curiosity. This man is shorter, though not by much, and a little younger. His eyes, heavy with eyeliner, are bright and inquisitive, but could never hold that same uncanny brilliance. I can't decide whether or not Bram would have rocked the neon green faux-fur coat.

'Sorry,' he says in a busy sing-song, 'we're not open to the public today. Summer only, Wednesdays and Saturdays.'

'Oh, I'm not –'

'If you want the farm shop, it's the entrance at the back. I can walk you round there if you like. I'm heading that way.'

'Er, thank you.'

His energy is breezy but forthright. I should have prepared better, thought about how to say what I need to say, whatever that may be. This is going badly. I could end up heading home with a red face and a bag of potatoes.

'I think we've met before,' he says as he struggles to close the heavy door. 'I'm Jack Moreton. Were you at Abby's party last weekend?'

'I'm afraid not,' I reply as politely as I can, trying not to appear flustered. 'My name's Flora. Flora Cotton.'

Jack freezes. A touch dramatically. 'You're kidding?'

I give him a look that says it would be a pretty weak joke, but he gazes back seriously.

'No, I'm not kidding,' I add.

'Do you have any ID with you?'

'ID?'

He's the one who's flustered now. 'If you really are Flora Cotton, I have something that belongs to you.'

I rummage in my bag to find my purse while Jack Moreton stares at me like he can't believe I'm real. All I have is my bank card, but it seems to suffice.

'Would you come with me?'

His hands tremble more than mine as he passes the card back. I can't imagine what he wants to show me, but I want to see the house, see if it gives me any hint of what might have happened to Bram, so I follow him inside.

The hall is subtly different again. There is still the same sweeping staircase and monochrome tiles, though now there's a kid's wooden tricycle and a set of colourful picture books scattered across them. Pallas Athene is wearing a pink feather boa and top hat.

'My sister's here with her kids this week.' Jack moves the tricycle aside, although it's not in our way. 'She's called Flora too. It's an old family name. I can't wait to tell her about you!'

I follow him towards the door in the corner. It's then that I notice the portrait. Bram, dressed and posed as a typical Georgian gentleman. There's a square building in the background, and he is standing beside an oak sapling that is barely as tall as he is. In his hand, he is holding some kind of golden cube.

'You made it,' I say quietly. It was all I wanted to know: did Bram make it back to his own time? It seems he did. Do I want to know any more?

'That's one of my ancestors, Abraham Moreton,' Jack tells me when he sees my interest in the picture. 'I look like him, don't you think?'

He pulls the same pose but with exaggerated exuberance, as though the golden cube weighs a tonne. I laugh.

'Yes, I can see a resemblance.'

'I took his name, as it happens. Professionally, I mean. Our family name is Stock now. Can you imagine? Jack Stock. Thump thump. I wanted the extra syllable and I thought, well, he's a handsome chap, why not?'

It's strange to see Bram in two dimensions, but I don't sigh or shake or do anything that might give away any particular emotion. I just look at him. He is older, with some grey at the temples and lines to his features, but it is an astonishing likeness.

'He was quite a character,' Jack continues. 'Left a whole series of predictions about the future, some of which made sense and some not so much. He predicted the First and Second World Wars accurately, but when he said, "In the year 1980, put your money in Apple," no one knew what he meant. My grandfather planted an orchard!'

I laugh again, unsure whether to believe him. I'm beginning to think Jack is a bit tricksy himself. I like his vibrant energy, though.

'That's the old Athenaeum behind him. It was a sort of fancy science club that used to be where the library is in town.'

'Oh yes?'

I smile inwardly to think that, until now, I've only seen it from the inside.

'Oh dear, I've gone into tour guide mode,' Jack grins, playing it up. 'If you would like to look at *this* picture over here, things get really interesting.'

I follow him to a portrait on the other side of the door. A woman. She is standing beside the same oak sapling as Bram and is also holding a cube in her hand. I know who she is, looking back at me through eyes that are in some ways familiar. Did she always appear that way to me? I want to like her despite the envy pricking my heart.

'This is Abraham's wife, Edith. The portrait caused a scandal at the time because the geometric shape in her hand symbolised discovery and completion, so the scientific community didn't approve of it being held by a woman. Similarly, with the Athenaeum in the background, it's sticking two fingers up at the establishment. They were pretty unconventional for their day.'

I picture the stuffy old men lining the staircase at the Athenaeum and can well imagine their disapproval. Good for Edith, sticking it to them.

'They were both scientists?'

'Yes. Their theory on ultraviolet wavelength was a forerunner of what eventually became quantum mechanics. I guess if you found a textbook old enough, they'd get a mention.'

Through the door, the study is chaotic, but in a different way from how I remember it. It's as if every issue of Vogue wandered in and exploded. There are racks of clothes in every colour: gowns and suits of silk and satin from brightest white to darkest midnight. Costumes from all over history: medieval pantaloons, flapper dresses, military uniforms. Necklaces and ruffs and boots and shoes. A wizard's hat of bright stars. A stage magician's cloak lined in blood red.

Jack makes another play of clearing a space to get to a shelf on the far wall, but it doesn't scratch the surface.

'Excuse the mess,' he says, rifling through boxes on the lower shelves. 'I'm starting a tour of Europe next week and can never decide what to take.'

'You're an actor?'

'Of course, darling! I take it you didn't catch my nude Hamlet at The Vaults, then?'

'I'm afraid not.'

He picks up a shoe box with triumph, only to find it empty and toss it over his shoulder.

'That's a shame. Four stars in *The London Standard.* They did a whole bit on "to bare or not to bare". It was pretty funny.'

'Well, that is the question,' I muse, which makes him chuckle as he climbs onto a precarious-looking chair to wrestle a further shoe box from the highest shelf.

'Aha, got it!'

Inside this shoe box is a smaller wooden box. Jack opens it to reveal yet another box. This one is much smaller and looks like the golden cube from the portraits of Bram and Edith. He hands it to me.

'In the year 2025, Flora Cotton will come to Wellsingham Hall. The gold box is hers. She is the only one who can open it.'

He says this with formality, as if recanting an oath, and I take it in both hands with the same sort of reverence. It's so heavy, it must be real gold. I don't know what it's supposed to mean. Is it a symbol? Something about Bram's work that he wants me to carry on?

'You were Abraham Moreton's final prediction, Flora. To be honest, everyone's had a go at opening the box over the years; it's been passed down for so many generations. Always intriguing and always impossible.'

'And it belongs to me?'

'Definitely. My dad looked into it years ago. He's a lawyer. A nasty one, too. He really wanted that weight of gold to be declared his own property. But the family lawyers were adamant that it belonged to Flora Cotton, who would retrieve it at the appropriate time. We were merely custodians.'

I stare at the box. We both do, absorbed in the moment.

Jack cracks first.

'Well open it!' he cries.

'But I don't…'

As I speak, I realise how to open the box. I hold my right hand over the top of it, and we are both startled by a mechanical click as a thin hinge opens the top edge.

'How did you do that?' Jack asks in wonder. 'Biometrics or something?'

'I have a key,' I reply with a grin.

Inside, there is a piece of rolled-up parchment. My bat pendant necklace is folded over the top of it, shimmering and lovely as ever. Hidden since yesterday for two hundred years.

I put the box down on top of a pile of clothes spilling from a tea chest and take the pendant in my hand. I hold it to my chest. My heart.

When I come to unroll the parchment, it is a letter written in old, spidery text.

Dearest Flora,

If you are reading this, then well done, things have played out as they should. I trust you will find your necklace safely enclosed and that you were not without it for too long.

I am an old man now and have struggled over the past decades to decide what to tell you. Suffice it to say that I have had a good, long life, but it is approaching its rightful conclusion. As you know, someone like me is not supposed to be forever.

I was able to take your advice to make Edith a part of my life. We had a happy marriage, welcoming five children into the world, and she was instrumental in helping me to channel my scientific interests. Edith grew to be a very capable scientist herself and was much cheered by my assertion that the future would hold better things for her sex.

Not a day has gone by that I have not thought of you, my beloved Flora. There are many days when I wish we could have remained ghosts forever.

I remain indebted to you, my love. Life takes so much from us, but it also bestows many gifts. I wish only good things for you. Don't look back.

Ever yours,
Bram

Jack has been trying to leave me in peace while I read, moving clothes, checking his nail polish, but I can tell he's intrigued to know what the note says. I don't share it.

'Is everything alright?' he asks.

'Yes.'

I could say something trite like *everything is as it should be*, but I don't feel that way. Not yet. I miss Bram so much, it feels like a physical ache. I miss him even more now, seeing his writing, reading his words in his beautiful voice. I hold my pendant and remember our time in the Bat Realm, in Lyrium, the Market of Pam Angra. I'm glad he had a good life, left a real legacy, but how I wish I could have lived that life with him.

'Not to be,' I whisper.

I roll up the parchment and seal it back within the gold box, which I push into my bag before putting on the necklace. The bat gem winks, happy to be back where it belongs.

'Oh. My. God!' Jack declares, the shimmering gem dislodging some vital thought. 'The Bat Girl! I knew you looked familiar.'

I look at him in surprise. 'Bat Girl?'

'Come on!'

He grabs my hand and virtually skips us back into the hallway, across the tiles to the lounge where golden wallpaper dazzles in the autumn sunlight.

'There!' he says, triumphant, pointing at a painting above another immense fireplace before clapping his hands, dancing with delight.

It's me. Or at least the finest rendering of me I could imagine. I'm seated on a velvet chaise wearing a black satin ball gown that falls just off my shoulders, my hair curled into ringlets. Over my left shoulder, two bats are hanging as though from the top of the picture, one larger than the other: Magda and Ralina. The present and the past. All here. All together.

'I bet an ancestor of yours knew Abraham Moreton. Wouldn't that be amazing?'

I want to tell him that it *was* amazing, all of it, but say nothing. Perhaps it was far too amazing to be real. That's for me alone to decide.

As I follow Jack to the door, he remains so excited by everything, like he doesn't want it to end.

'Why don't you stay for lunch? We could go to the farm shop for a sandwich?'

An old conversation strays through the sunlight towards me, the smell of salted almonds, the sound of a merry crowd by the river. *I'll never make you a sandwich.* I picture a ball of cotton candy falling through a gap in a board. A hole in time. A dream or a memory. What's the difference, really? If I stay here, that's all there will ever be.

'That would be lovely, but I need to get back to town.'

'My van's outside. Please, let me run you there.'

Jack's got his hands together as if praying, bobbing like a child who wants a toy. I'm happy to walk to the bus stop, figure out what happens next, but he's so relentless that I can't resist.

'Okay. Thank you.'

'Amazing! Photo first, though.'

Before I can move away, Jack puts his arm around me and holds up his phone to take a photograph of us standing in the hallway. I look awkward, eyes half closed, but he is poised, face angled to best capture his photogenic features.

Over my shoulder, Bram watches the scene with indulgent dismay.

21

'So this is where you work, Bat Girl?' Jack asks as we pull up outside the library. He's called me that several times on the journey, and I'm surprised not to mind.

'For now,' I reply. I look at the castellated tower in the low autumn sun, the rose window dulled in silhouette. 'It won't be here much longer, but I'm thinking about moving on in any case.'

'What will you do?'

'I'm not sure. I've been thinking about travelling, seeing a bit more of the world.'

'Excellent! I've got literally thousands of cousins all over the world you'll be able to stay with.'

I shake my head. 'I doubt they'll welcome a stranger turning up.'

'A stranger? Are you kidding? You're Flora Cotton. *The* Flora Cotton. You actually showed up! Do you know how famous you are?'

'Famous? What do you –'

'Seriously, our family socials are on fire today!'

He turns his phone screen to me and scrolls back up a feed of hearts and surprised face emojis and 'wow!' and 'OMG!', up to the photo of us in the hallway that started the thread. The Moreton descendants are certainly an expressive bunch.

'You can start by coming on my tour with me,' Jack continues. It's not a question. It's not even an idea. It's a fact.

'What do you mean? I can't go on your tour. What would I do?'

'Whatever you want. Act. Paint. Write poetry. Dance on tables. Take photos of donkeys and wrinkly old men. Find a man as handsome as Abraham Moreton to squire you about.'

I look back at him with question marks, blushing. He returns my look through narrowed lashes.

'I saw you eyeing him up, girl!'

The portrait. I laugh, not a polite chuckle but an actual shriek of a laugh. I've chuckled away at pretty much everything Jack has said today. He's a funny guy, but this is priceless. I won't be able to explain why, but I laugh until tears are running down my face. Until it's painful. Until he tells me to stop, looks confused.

'You're not a lunatic, are you?' he asks as my laughter trails off into ragged breaths. I can still feel it in my gut, shaking my speech.

'Honestly, I don't know!'

'Well, let's hope so! Oh, say you'll come to Europe with me! We're doing Paris, Berlin, Prague, Athens, then back to London, Dublin and Edinburgh. It'll be amazing!'

'Edinburgh?'

'Of course, we have a two-week run at Summerhall. Please, Flora? It's very hard to say no to Jack Moreton, you know. I was one of those kids who can hold their breath until they pass out. It's how I got out of training as a lawyer.'

I look at the library. From here, I can make out the square edges of the Athenaeum skirting the castellated façade. The palimpsest.

'When were you last abroad?' he persists.

I assume he's not counting worlds between worlds.

'Never.'

'You've never been abroad? Jeezus! That settles it. You just leave it all to Jack. Well, Jack's agent. We leave a week on Thursday.'

I watch Jack's animated features dance as he speaks, so similar to Bram in so many ways, yet so very different. Old words echo softly: *A better question would be, can you leave the library?*

'But why, Jack? Why would you want to take me with you? You don't know me from anyone, I'm nothing but a weird footnote in your family's history.'

He shrugs. 'I'm not sure. I suppose I feel a connection to you. Not in *that* way, obviously! But it's strange, as if someone is whispering in my ear, saying *look after this girl, get her moving*.' He scratches his face, briefly thoughtful. 'Maybe I'm the lunatic.'

I look from Jack to the library. I can't stop smiling.

'Jack, it doesn't sound strange at all.'

That evening, I walk home through the park and sit on a bench that I've never sat on before. It's not too cold, but Autumn always likes to bite a little. I watch a wind-rushed cluster of brittle leaves glide along the walkway and listen to the distant, tinny tunes of the young teenagers hanging out on the bandstand. The yappy dogs and clumsy pigeons. Life continuing.

When I called my mum earlier, we talked for quite a while. I thought she would be more *I told you so* about The Black Eyed Boy, or guilt-trip me about not calling, but she was mostly excited that I'll be visiting sometime soon. She sounds happy with the werewolf (I should start calling him

Cyril), and has even got a job as a tour guide. She'll be good at that, spreading sunshine.

I told her about the library closing, but decided not to say anything about Bram. I'm not sure how much I want to share the part of him that was mine. I'm not even sure how I could.

Looking back towards town, I can see the oak tree from Bram's portrait, the sapling now towering over every other tree in the park. The library isn't visible through the elms and beeches that line the edge of the road, but I can just make out the shadow of the taller Athenaeum through the wispy tree tops.

I won't come back to town much in the years to come, but whenever I do, I will sit here and look over at that oak tree. I will think of Bram. Sometimes I will picture Edith with him, but he will usually be alone. Sometimes a tiny bat will flitter around him and land in his palm. He will say something to her, and they will both look over at me. I will know they are content.

Then there will be times when I throw off my coat and run across the silvered lawn to him. It is always night when this happens, and the stars, ancient and watchful, will bless us, for even stars cannot endure without romance.

On those nights, Bram will take my hands, hold me tight, and we will dance our hearts to life once more across the frozen sky.

AUTHOR'S NOTE

The Unravelling of Flora Cotton was written during a time when the library in my hometown, King's Lynn, really was being moved to a converted car park. The old library, the Gothic-style Carnegie Building, was gifted to the people of King's Lynn in 1905, taken over by the council in 1974, and then, in 2025, repurposed for community use by a cultural charity. Many locals remain strongly connected to the building and believe it belongs to the people of the town.

The old library building was the inspiration for this story, though they differ slightly. The real building had only one public floor, so no mezzanine or spooky basement, and it wasn't built on the site of the old Athenaeum, which stood across the road from what is now the new library.

But it was full of ghosts – and countless doors to amazing worlds.

ACKNOWLEDGEMENTS

Many thanks first to the brilliant Sue Burge for all of her editing and mentoring support.

John Chandler did a fantastic job of making the finished article tangible and beautiful. Thank you.

Thanks to everyone who helped and inspired me to get the words out, especially Alison Dunhill, Pam Greenwood, Fliss Cary, everyone at Wisbech Stanza Group, and my family: Mary, Robert, and James.

Finally, thanks to Ben Wood, whose love and support made everything possible.

NOTES AND ATTRIBUTIONS

Quotes from *The Count of Monte Cristo* are from the Project Gutenberg eBook version.

Lyric excerpts from *Nights in White Satin* (Justin Hayward) and *Call It Stormy Monday* (T-Bone Walker) are quoted with appreciation.

The line beginning 'And the gods did honour Alcestis' is from Plato's *Symposium*.

ABOUT THE AUTHOR

Tracee grew up on RAF bases in East Anglia and lived all over the UK before returning to King's Lynn, Norfolk, in 2018.

Her first poetry pamphlet, *Broken Passages*, was independently published in 2023. *Stone Trees*, a poetry and image collaboration with artist Fliss Cary, was published by Atomic Bohemian in 2024.

The Unravelling of Flora Cotton is Tracee's first novel. She previously self-published a YA e-book novella, *Where I Find You*, in 2015.

ABOUT LYRIA BOOKS

Founded in 2025, Lyria Books is an independent publisher of darkly romantic fiction and poetry. Head to lyriabooks.co.uk for more details.